W9-BLE-505

This photograph of Casita and her brother, Jack,
was taken at the Carlisle Indian Industrial School around 1879.

HIDDEN HISTORIES

THE LOST ONES

MICHAELA MacCOLL

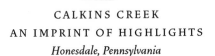

CALKINS CREEK
AN IMPRINT OF HIGHLIGHTS
Honesdale, Pennsylvania

Text copyright © 2016 by Michaela MacColl
Cover illustration copyright © 2016 by Mark Summers

All rights reserved.
For information about permission to reproduce selections from this book,
contact permissions@highlights.com.

Although this work centers around characters who are actual persons, about
whom limited facts are known, this is a work of fiction. Names, characters, and
incidents are products of the author's imagination and are used fictitiously.

Calkins Creek
An Imprint of Highlights
815 Church Street
Honesdale, Pennsylvania 18431

Printed in the United States of America
ISBN: 978-1-62091-625-4 (hardcover)
ISBN: 978-1-62979-742-7 (e-book)
Library of Congress Control Number: 2016936345

First edition
The text of this book is set in Garamond 3.
Design by Barbara Grzeslo
Production by Sue Cole
10 9 8 7 6 5 4 3 2 1

THIS BOOK IS DEDICATED TO

SANTOS CASTRO ROMERO—

NDÉ NANTA' ÁN SHIMA'

WHOSE ORAL HISTORIES PRESERVE

THE LOST ONES.

DANIEL CASTRO ROMERO, JR., MSW, MA

GENERAL COUNCIL CHAIRMAN

LIPAN APACHE BAND OF TEXAS

MAX AND MADI,

WHO I THINK WOULD BE JUST AS BRAVE.

—*MM*

"LET IT BE A CAMPAIGN OF ANNIHILATION, OBLITERATION AND COMPLETE DESTRUCTION."

*—Orders received by the 4th US Cavalry about the
Indian problem in South Texas
Spring 1873*

THE CUELCAHEN NDÉ: CASTRO FAMILY CREST
by Daniel Castro Romero, Jr., Ndé Nanta' án (meaning leader or chief)

Casita and Jack, were members of the Castro Family. The Castro family crest is a modern one, designed after interviewing various family members who identified the following icons as having cultural and historical meaning.

Circle
The circle with four arrows pointing in each of the four directions—North, South, East, and West—represents the Circle of Life. The northern quarter represents mother earth, the eastern quarter represents fire and the sun's life-giving light, the southern quarter represents water, and the western quarter represents wind.

Star
The five-pointed star symbol represents the Northern Star, which the Ndé used to guide them in nighttime travels.

Crescent Moon
To the Ndé, the crescent moon symbol represents the guardian spirits of the night. The crescent moon also symbolizes the moon's resting place.

Three Peaks
The three peaks under the crescent moon symbol represent the highest mountains in Texas, the Guadalupe peaks.

Three Straight Lines
The three lines under the three peaks each represent a river. The first line represents the Sabine River, the second line represents the Red River, and the third line represents the Rio Grande River.

The Sun
There are five rays on the sun, one for each of the directions and the fifth represents the horizon.

Three Arrows
The three arrows represent the three directions from which many of our people fled. They crossed three rivers (the Rio Grande, the Red River, and Sabine River) to protect their families. Note that the arrows have fletching (feathers) only on one side to honor the many families who were split up. We will add a fourth arrow when the US government recognizes the Lipan Band.

Three Wavy Lines
The lines represent the Gulf of Mexico.

PART ONE

Nde'

GLOSSARY

Ndé (pronounced En-day): The name the Lipan Apache call
themselves.

Cuelcahen Ndé (People of the Tall Grass): The name of the
particular band of Apaches in this novel.

Indaa: The name the Lipan Apache have for the white
settlers and soldiers. Soldiers are also called "bluebellies,"
because of their dark blue uniforms.

wickiup: A round hut with walls made of buffalo skins and a
roof of branches and mud.

Usen: The Apache name for God.

Nde'

CHAPTER ONE

El Día de Los Gritos (The Day of Screams), 1877
El Remolino, Mexico

D AWN WAS COMING, BUT NOT YET. CASITA SAW A THIN RIM of gold over the mountains to the east. The moon was setting on the opposite side of the sky. From her perch on top of the enormous boulder, she looked down to the river valley and saw their village, nestled on the shore of the river. Mist floated up from the cool water.

Downstream, moving silently, a long line of raiders on horseback traveled purposefully among the clouds. Her father was at the head of the line. Just before he turned round the bend of the river, he twisted his neck to look up at her perch. He half lifted his hand in a salute. He knew she would be watching him; it was their secret. Casita hugged herself tightly. She would have loved to jump up on the rock, wave wide, and send him off properly—but she knew better. He would scold her for making herself a target—standing tall, visible to the enemy. Her people, the Ndé, were always in danger and even the smallest child learned to protect herself.

Once the sun came up, Casita's mother would expect her back. She slithered down the rock on her stomach, her toes finding the hidden ridges to support her weight. Her little brother, Jack, often begged her, his face angry, to tell him how to get up on the boulder. "No," she would always say. "It's my private place."

A few feet above the ground, she pushed off the rock and landed in a crouch. Her leather moccasins with their turned-up toes protected her feet from the sharp stones. Hurrying down the steep slope, she made her way back to the village. She had an armful of wild onions to explain her absence. They were the first of the season and Mother loved them.

In the mist coming off the river, the village was at first only hazy shapes of the occasional round wickiups and pointed teepees. Her wickiup was on the farthest edge of the village and closest to her. Casita could remember when her mother had started to build the wickiup. She knew then that they would stay in one place for a while. The thatched roof and buffalo skin walls had sheltered them for several seasons.

Casita hurried to check the agave hearts roasting under a huge mound, as tall as her head. The day before, the women of the village had harvested the spiked agave cacti and trimmed them down to the hearts. They had prepared a hole in the ground and lined it with baking stones. Casita had been chosen to go in the hole and build a fire to heat the stones. Once the fire had died, the hearts had been thrown in the pit, then covered with wet grasses and dirt. The hearts would roast underground until they were tender and sweet. She sniffed. Among the scents of mist and river mud, she could make out the delicious smell. Casita placed her hand on top of the mound. It was still warm. Mother would want them to roast a little longer. Her stomach rumbled, thinking of the feast there would be when the hearts were dug up.

Casita thought she'd better find herself a new task before she got another one she might not care for. She built a fire in the ring of stones, spinning a wooden stick into a hollow filled with tinder until she made a spark. She wished her mother wasn't so stubborn about using matches the Indaa, the white men, had invented. It would be easier. As soon as the fire had caught and was burning well, Casita slid the cooking stone onto the rocks so it rested above the fire. She laid the onions in a row on the stone to let them cook.

Stooping because she was so tall, her mother lifted the hide door and emerged from the wickiup. Casita always felt tiny next to her. She rested a hand for a moment on top of Casita's head, her usual morning greeting. As a married woman, she wore her hair loose about her shoulders. Her buckskin tunic reached the tops of her moccasins. Buckskin was heavy and smelly in the heat of the day, but Mother refused to use the Indaa's cotton cloth. Casita wished she would change her mind; she liked the cotton skirts the other girls wore.

Mother sniffed, catching the smell of the onions right

away. Casita thought she was pleased. "We needed that for the stew today." She took a hard look at Casita. "Why is your hair is so untidy?" She undid Casita's loosened braid and redid it so it hung flat on Casita's back. Then she asked casually, "Did you watch your father leave from your rock?"

Casita's head jerked up. "You know about my secret place?"

Her mother nodded, smiling slightly. "Everyone needs a place to be alone; sometimes, we need silence to hear our own thoughts."

Casita felt a pang of recognition in her heart; Mother was saying something Casita had always known but didn't know how to say. "You never said anything before."

"You work hard. I don't mind that you go off alone sometimes." Mother tugged on her daughter's braid and easily lowered herself to sit next to Casita. "But you won't always have the time for such indulgences. You'll be a woman of the tribe soon."

Her words made Casita shiver. Looking about to make sure they were alone, Casita said, "Mother, what if I don't want to become a woman yet?"

Mother laughed, a sound that Casita rarely heard. "Daughter, you have no choice."

"But what if I'm not strong enough for the ceremony?" The Changing Woman ceremony was four days of fasting, meditating, and dancing. Mother would work for months to collect the food for all the guests and the gifts they would give in honor of Casita becoming a woman. It was the most important ceremony that Casita would ever be part of—but what if she couldn't do it?

"You will be ready," Mother promised. "And the ceremony changes everything. During mine, the Changing Woman Goddess came to me. I felt as though I could fly. It will be the same for you." Her mother touched her only jewelry, a necklace with a small mirror surrounded by blue sky stones. "My mother gave me this after my ceremony. Perhaps I will give it to you."

Casita's fingers went to the shell that hung on a strip of leather around her neck. "Your necklace is very pretty, but I love this," she said. "Father gave it to me."

"You can wear more than one necklace, you know." Her mother smiled. "You will still be his daughter after the ceremony."

Casita thought about her father riding away, weapons ready. "He'll come home safely, won't he?"

"Of course. He is very brave and very clever."

"But the Indaa are fierce fighters," Casita said.

Mother nodded. "They hate us."

"Father told me we did not always fight them," Casita said slowly.

"When they first came, they were not so greedy. We sometimes helped each other, especially when we had the same enemy."

Her mother did not need to name the Comanche. Every Ndé child knew the Comanche were their greatest foes.

"But the Indaa are greedy." Mother's voice was quiet, but

Casita could hear the anger in it. "They want everything: all the land, all the water, all the buffalo. We stand in their way, so now they hunt us."

"They won't come to Mexico, though," Casita reassured herself. "We're far away from the land they want."

"It's forty miles to the great river that is the border. The Texans aren't welcome here, so we can stay and prosper. So long as we can offer the Mexicans cheap horses, they will protect us."

Casita counted in her mind the summers they had spent at El Remolino. Two, no, three so far. They hadn't stayed in one place for as long in her whole life. "Will we stay here forever?"

Mother shrugged. "The hunting is good. Our corn grows well. The river gives us clean water. If the Army stays on their side of the great river . . ." She did not need to finish the sentence.

"That's why Father has to ride so far to find a good fight." Jack spoke from the entry to the wickiup. He wore only buckskin breeches and he was rubbing the sleep from his eyes. His face was streaked with dirt.

Mother made an exasperated noise when she saw him. Rising effortlessly, she dipped a rag in a gourd of clean water to scrub his face. He complained, but she paid him no mind. "How do you find so much dirt?" she asked as she rubbed her cloth on his bald skull. Jack, like the other boys, shaved his head except for his long tail of hair that sprouted from the top of his head. Jack shook his head irritably.

Casita started to giggle. Jack scowled at her. "What are you laughing at?" he asked.

"You look just like your pony when a fly is pestering him. He swats his tail around too," Casita said.

Mother smiled and continued to scrub.

"You would not talk to me like that if I was a warrior," Jack said. "When I grow up, I'm going to raid with Father and show the Indaa that they can't take our land. I will steal more horses than any raider has ever stolen. We will be rich."

"We only steal the horses to trade with the Mexicans for safety. We have no use for more horses than we need," Mother said calmly. "You want glory and wealth. That is why it will be many summers before your father lets you join a raid. The Ndé fight only to survive. And if we can survive without fighting, that is what we will do."

"Even if we had to live on a reservation?" Casita asked. They had come to Mexico rather than be confined to a plot of land the United States government chose.

"That is not living at all. But the best living is when we can be peaceful here, growing our food and watching our children grow." Mother moved away to check the agave hearts.

Jack crouched next to the fire, warming his hands at the flame. Quietly, so Mother couldn't hear, Jack said, "I bet Father would say differently. He would say to fight to the death. He needs me in the raiding party. Aren't I the best wrestler in the band? Aren't I the one who can keep the burning sage on my skin the longest?" The boys of the tribe

17

trained in many ways to be strong fighters. The burning sage taught them to withstand pain without crying out.

"You are still a little boy," Casita said. "Father will not let you fight for many seasons yet. I will be a woman before you are a warrior."

Jack grimaced at his sister, while his arm snaked out to snatch a wild onion. But Casita was wise to his tricks, and just as fast she smacked his fingers away. Before he could retaliate, their mother's voice interrupted, "The horses need watering."

"I'll do it," said Casita, quickly getting to her feet. It was stifling next to the fire, even in the cool morning air. When the sun started to rise the heat would be unbearable.

"It's my job," Jack cried, unwilling to give up time with his beloved pony.

Mother's eyes went to the fire and the baking stone where the onions were starting to smoke. Casita sighed and returned to the fire to poke at the singed greens. Jack grabbed an onion before she could stop him, and he took off running toward the river.

The sun rose higher and the rest of the village woke up. With no set pattern to their mornings, everyone did what needed to be done. All the able men were with Father on the raid; only the elderly, women, and children remained. Jack and the other boys pretended they were the protectors of the tribe while the warriors were away—but where would any real danger come from? The village was safe enough.

Finally Casita decided the onions were ready and she moved them to a clay plate to cool. The round baking stone,

18

empty for the moment, seemed to be calling to her. She found a dried cattail among the kindling. She dipped the furry head into a clay pot of water and began quickly drawing a figure on the hot stone. As the wet cattail met the stone, it sizzled and spat. Two parallel lines, connected by a rounded one—and she had a horse's head. The image remained for just a few seconds before it steamed away. Casita smiled and tried again. This time she managed the whole horse before the image faded.

"Was that a coyote?" The voice startled her. She looked around to see her cousin Juanita watching her with solemn eyes. Juanita was a few summers younger than Casita, but they were close friends. Juanita held the hand of her little brother, Miguel. He wobbled as he stood; he was only a few weeks out of his cradleboard.

"It was a horse," Casita retorted. "Not that it lasted very long."

"Maybe you should draw with this. It might last longer," Juanita said, offering a long stick with a charred end.

"Thank you." Casita smiled at her favorite cousin. A few swipes of the stick and she had a warrior on his horse, sitting tall with a bow and arrow strapped to his back. Her father.

"I like that one," Juanita whispered.

Mother appeared. She frowned when she saw what was in Casita's hand. "You are too old to be playing instead of working. You must put away your toys."

"But the onions are finished," Casita protested.

"We'll need more tomorrow." Mother came closer and examined the baking stone. A smile flitted across her lips when she saw Casita's horse and rider. Her voice was a touch softer when she said, "Take yourselves off and find some more onions."

"Both of us?" Casita asked.

"Juanita should know where they are, too," her mother said.

Casita leapt to her feet and hurried away before Mother changed her mind. She led Juanita up the hill to the plateau overlooking the camp and river. During the last part of the walk, Casita had to carry little Miguel on her hip. Up here they could see past the bend in the river to where Jack was watering his pony, Choya. Directly below, they looked down at the busy camp. Mother was in front of the wickiup beating a skin with her special rock and scraping away the hair so the skin would be smooth. Then she would dye it yellow before making it into Casita's Changing Woman ceremony dress. She had already started collecting food and gifts for the ceremony.

Casita looked away and sighed. Her mother's words had helped to calm her fears about the ceremony. Every other Ndé woman had managed it, so Casita could certainly do it, too. Still, she was nervous. And what about afterward? As far as she could tell, being a woman of the tribe meant shouldering responsibility for everything: cooking, foraging, clothing, children, houses. It seemed that the men only had to hunt and fight. She would rather stay a child and have time she could call her own.

"Can you show me the steps to the dance of your ceremony?" Juanita asked, meaning the last dance, when Casita would twirl around with her cane. The purpose was to show the band she was physically fit to be a woman of the tribe. She would wear eagle feathers and her face would be dusted with pollen. The Goddess would bless her and then Casita would bless all the members of the tribe in return. Maybe Mother was right and the ceremony would be worth all the preparations.

Juanita was too little to understand Casita's doubts, and Casita would not burden her cousin with them. Instead she would dance. She looked around for sticks to serve as canes. Finding two, she gave one to Juanita.

"I will show you," Casita said. "But you have to dance, too. In a few summers this will be your dance." They sat Miguel against a rock to watch. Then Casita started to dance, thumping the stick against the rock to set the rhythm. Her feet had long ago memorized the steps. Juanita mimicked every step. Soon they were dancing wildly until they were both out of breath and laughing. Miguel giggled so hard he fell over and couldn't right himself without Juanita's help.

They tossed their make-believe canes aside and flopped down on the ground to recover. After a brief silence, Juanita asked, "Is it true that during the ritual you will be able to heal the sick?"

It seemed impossible that any ritual could really give someone as ordinary as herself magical powers. Finally Casita answered, "I don't know. We'll know soon enough. Both of us."

Content with that answer, Juanita was quiet. The sun was

partway along its journey and it was getting hotter. A breeze from the other side of the river carried the sound of horse hooves striking stone. Casita sat up. Could it be her father returning so soon? Had something terrible happened? Her eyes scanned the river. There was no one. None of the people in the camp below seemed to have heard anything. Perhaps she had imagined it.

Suddenly a bugle sounded across the valley. A gunshot cracked the air. A second shot and then a third. Casita threw herself flat on the ground and crawled to the edge to see. At the crest of the rising hill across the river, a row of soldiers appeared, the sun at their backs. Hundreds of them, wearing the blue woolen uniform of the US Cavalry. To the sound of a merry bugle, the soldiers charged straight for her home.

Nde'

CHAPTER TWO

CROUCHED ON THE LEDGE, CASITA COULDN'T MOVE, COULDN'T tear her eyes away. Although the soldiers were across the river, their noise was deafening. They were shouting and wildly shooting their guns into the air. She heard yells from the village; they knew danger was coming.

Juanita crawled out to look. She cried out when she saw the soldiers. "The Americans aren't allowed here!" Juanita gasped.

"They came anyway!" Casita answered.

"We have to tell the village!" Juanita stood up to warn them.

Casita pulled Juanita to the ground. "Stay down! They know!" She forced her fear deep inside herself; she was responsible for Juanita and her brother. Helpless, they watched the confusion below. The women were trying to gather their children. Old men ran out of their huts, some not even dressed. They had no weapons, while every soldier carried a saber, a gun, and a bandolier of precious ammunition.

"Look!" Juanita pointed across the river. "There are even more up there." Another group of soldiers was massed in the distance, at the top of the long slope leading to the village.

"They are waiting for their turn to attack," Casita whispered. "There are too many." The Ndé had never faced such an enemy. If only her father were still here. Without the men, the village didn't stand a chance against so many. Her family, her friends, were as good as dead. Or worse, taken prisoner.

But wait! Jack was free. She crawled to the western edge of the plateau. Her eyes searched desperately for her brother with the horses, around the bend of the river, out of sight from the camp. He must have heard the gunshots; he was swinging his body onto the back of his pony and galloping toward the camp.

"No," she shouted. "Run away, Jack! There are too many . . ." But her words were like tiny specks of dust in a storm. Her brother couldn't possibly hear her. She crawled back from the ledge, dragging Juanita with her.

How could she help her people? She couldn't. But she could make sure Juanita and her brother lived. And then try to help her own brother. After that, all Casita could do was stay alive.

24

"What do we do?" Juanita asked, her eyes fixed on Casita.

Casita picked Miguel up and thrust him into Juanita's arms.

"Take Miguel and hide!" Casita ordered. "You know where!" Around every Ndé camp were places to go to ground, to keep safe from their enemies. Even the smallest child knew what to do.

"Come with us!" Juanita cried. Her hold on Miguel was so tight he began to cry.

"I have to help my brother! Keep Miguel quiet!" Casita shouted over her shoulder as she started down the slope. She slipped on the gravel, but she dared not slow. She must catch Jack before he charged into the camp. There were too many; he would be killed. But if she could catch him and convince him to run, they could gallop as fast as they could, into the desert where the bluebellies couldn't track them.

She heard hooves splashing from the south. Stumbling, almost falling, she leapt in front of him as he came round the bend. "Stop!" she shouted.

Jack dragged the pony's head to one side just in time to keep Casita from being trampled. Choya reared and Jack slid toward the pony's tail, spinning his arms to keep his balance.

"Get out of the way, Sister!" he panted. He had smeared river mud on his face and chest like war paint. "We're being attacked!"

"It's the American soldiers. Hundreds of them!" she shouted back. "I saw them." She pointed up toward the ridge.

Now she had Jack's attention. "They must have known Father and the men were away on a raid."

Casita nodded; it made sense. But as Jack gathered himself to take off, she tried to catch hold of the pony's mane to stop him. "We have to run."

His face hardened and it was no longer a little boy staring down at her. Jack had become a warrior. "The Ndé don't run away!"

"To live, we do!" she cried. "They have guns. You'll be killed." Even as she said it, she knew it was no use. Jack wouldn't miss his first chance to fight for their people.

"You go. I'll defend our family. It's what Father would want."

"Father would want us to live," Casita shouted.

"What about Mother?" he demanded.

As he said it, Jack's anger was winning over Casita's common sense. How dare these soldiers attack their home and family? How could they run and leave Mother to die or be captured? Without saying a word, she pulled her knife from its sheath at her waist and stretched out her other hand to Jack. He grabbed her forearm and hauled her up behind him. She was barely astride the pony before Jack urged it on at a gallop toward the village. Casita's arm tightened around Jack's waist. His skin was slick with sweat; she could smell the fear and salt on him. His back tensed and he let out a war cry worthy of their father.

The soldiers were at the other end of the camp from their wickiup.

"We're in time," she said in his ear.

"No, we aren't," he said, pointing at a soldier riding toward them hard. He was a big man, with a bushy mustache. The sun was shining in Casita's eyes and she couldn't make out his face.

All the other noises faded to nothing and all they heard was the soldier's long whoops and the pounding of his horse's hooves. At first Casita thought he was heading toward them, but then she realized he was intent on a defiant figure. Her mother.

She stood in front of their wickiup, an axe in her hand. Tall and fierce, she hollered a war cry of her own, daring the soldier to fight her. Casita felt a thrill of pride; this was what it was to be Ndé!

Jack swung the pony's body between them. Casita tumbled off and hurried to her mother. The soldier dismounted, too. He didn't call for help. A woman and two children did not frighten him, Casita saw. He would soon learn that Ndé women and children knew how to fight.

Jack leapt off his pony. His lips drawn and his teeth bared, he gripped his knife, pointing it downward.

The soldier pushed him aside to reach Mother. Jack ducked under his arm and stabbed the soldier in his side. With a yowl of pain, the soldier whirled back and brought the butt of his rifle onto Jack's head. Casita's brother fell hard to the ground and lay motionless. The soldier paused and knelt down to see if Jack were still alive.

Casita started to run to him, but her mother held her

back. Mother's eyes were wild, as though they did not see Casita. "No, daughter," she cried. "If he's not dead, they will take him. He is gone. You must run!"

"Only if you come with me!"

With a last look toward Jack, Mother grabbed her hand and they started running. If they could reach the safety of the hills, they could hide. They might live.

Casita tripped and fell. Her mother tried to pull her to her feet, but Casita's ankle buckled underneath her and she fell again.

"Stay down!" her mother ordered, standing in front of her, brandishing her axe. The soldier was staggering after them, holding his side where Jack had stabbed him. His pistol was in his hand. Mother cried out, but Casita couldn't make out her words. The soldier slowed. At first she thought her mother's words had turned him back, but no. He raised the pistol and aimed it at Mother.

"Run, Mother!" Casita begged. "Save yourself!"

Her mother didn't say a word; she just planted her feet to brace herself. What good would that do against a bullet? The soldier barked an order. Casita knew some English. He was telling Mother to drop the axe.

Casita pleaded in Ndé, "Drop the axe, Mother. Please. The soldiers will have us, but we'll be together."

Her mother's eyes didn't leave the soldier. Almost as though it were a prayer, she muttered, "They must not take us. Better to die than live on a reservation." Mother's lips twisted and she tightened her grip on the axe.

Suddenly a shot rang out and Mother's body jerked. As Casita looked up from the ground, a black hole appeared in the center of her mother's stomach and a crimson stain spread in all directions.

"Mother!" Casita cried as she crawled to where her mother had fallen. Casita pressed against the wound, but there was too much bleeding. Tears flowing down her cheeks, she buried her head against her mother's chest. The fighting around them seemed to fade, the sound of bullets hushed.

"Daughter." Her mother's voice stopped Casita's crying. "Close your eyes. I don't want you to see."

"Mother!"

"Close your eyes!"

Casita obeyed. Suddenly, there was a terrible blow to her forehead. She opened her eyes but they were full of blood. Was this what a bullet felt like?

Throwing up her arms to ward off another attack, she cried, "Mother! Help me!"

A second blow to her shoulder brought only darkness.

Nde'

CHAPTER THREE

Pain. Smoke. Casita did not want to come back from the blackness. Reluctantly she opened her eyes. She tried to push herself up, but her head exploded in a burst of searing pain. Touching her forehead, she felt blood. Not only her head, but her shoulders, too, were covered with blood. Why wasn't she dead?

As she forced herself to sit up, a wave of nausea swept through her. She retched into the dirt until her stomach was empty. When she was able to raise her head again, she could see the battle was over. Bodies lay everywhere. But she didn't spot a single dead soldier. They were all Ndé.

"Fire the village!" The loud command in English was echoed by one soldier to another. Casita's father had brought her to the American forts when she was younger. He had been proud of how quickly she had learned English. But now, she wished she didn't understand the soldiers' orders.

30

Two sets of boots came running past her. They were young boys, just barely men, and they were chattering like magpies. Carrying torches, they cheered as they put the flames to the dried grasses of the wickiups, including her own.

One boy stepped back to survey his handiwork and stumbled against the mound of dirt over the agave hearts.

"Caleb, there's something under here!" the boy hollered to his friend.

They both dug, the loose dirt easy to shift. All the while, they glanced back to the battlefield as if to be sure they weren't seen. The first boy put his hand in and pulled out a roasted agave heart. He yelped as it burned his fingers. Casita knew if things were different, she would laugh at the greedy boys looking for treasure in a roasting pit. But for now, all she could think of was how hard the women had worked to build the oven. And now no one would ever eat the agave hearts.

All the wickiups and teepees were burning. The soldiers were going to leave nothing. Her stomach twisted when she saw soldiers toss a body into the flames. Everywhere she looked it was like having a piece of her heart shredded. Her aunts and uncles and cousins. The children, too. Having gotten rid of one body, the solders went back for another. It was . . . efficient. Death was awful enough, but to be burned without ritual was even worse. She let tears flow down her cheeks—it was the only thing she could do to honor her people.

Soon the soldiers would come for her, too; she had to think of herself now. If she could reach the hills, she might survive. She began crawling, trying to keep her pounding head as still as she could.

"Jeremiah, there's one," Caleb said to the other boy.

She held herself motionless like a hare trying to deceive a coyote. She was sure they had spotted her. But the footsteps stopped at a woman's body a dozen steps from her. The woman lay limp, her long hair trailing on the ground. The boys picked her up, one taking the feet, the other her shoulders. A mirrored pendant fell from the body's neck, suspended by a thin strip of leather. She shook her head. No. It couldn't be. It must not be Mother. Mother wasn't a body. Even if she wore Mother's necklace and a buckskin dress, with a crimson stain spread across the front.

Caleb tore the necklace away and stowed it in his pocket. They brought the body to the burning hut and tossed it in.

Casita heard a low mournful sound grow louder and louder. The awful noise was coming from her own mouth. "Mother!" she cried. "No, Mother!"

Caleb and Jeremiah turned, looking for the source of the sound. Casita clapped her hand over her lips, but it was too late.

"There's a live one!" Caleb cried. They came running over to Casita, Jeremiah pulling a pistol from a holster at his hip. His hand shook as he aimed the gun at her.

"It's just a little girl," Jeremiah complained, but there was relief in his voice.

"She's hurt bad," Caleb said. "We could save ourselves some trouble and just throw her on the fire."

Casita tried to crawl away, though her head was swimming

32

in pain. Caleb grabbed her feet and pulled her back.

"It's almost like she understands us," Jeremiah laughed.

Casita knew she mustn't reveal she knew English. She mustn't lose the only advantage she had, no matter how tempting.

"What should we do with her?" Jeremiah asked.

Before Caleb could answer, they were interrupted. "You two! Is that girl alive?" A soldier had come up from behind them. He was familiar. Nursing a limp and pressing his hand to his side, Casita remembered how Jack had stabbed him. Her lips twisted in a smile; at least her brother had drawn blood. At least one soldier had paid a price for what they had done to her people.

Caleb nudged her with his boot. She curled up, trying to protect herself. "She's hurt bad," he said.

The soldier looked more closely at Casita. "I remember that one."

"Did you do this to her, Sergeant?" Jeremiah jibed. "She's awfully little for you to fight, ain't she?"

With his free hand, the soldier cuffed Jeremiah's head. "I didn't touch the girl—one of her own did that."

Before Casita could work out what that meant, the soldier went on. "Captain Carter wants as many Apache prisoners as we can carry—so take her to the sawbones and get her fixed up for the ride back."

"She might not make it, Sergeant."

He shrugged. "Then she dies on the road."

As the boys picked her up, Casita didn't resist—she felt as

33

though all her strength had flowed out into the dirt. Mother had died rather than be taken prisoner. What would she want Casita to do now? What could she do?

Although he was as skinny as a sapling grown too fast, Caleb still lifted her easily off the ground. His blue coat, unbuttoned to the waist, smelled of smoke, sweat, and dirty wool. Her stomach churned and if she'd had anything left to throw up, she would have.

He brought her past a group of prisoners, huddled together and under guard. Her mind eased when she saw Jack. He was alive. She stretched out her hand to him but he ignored her, the flames of their home reflected in his dark eyes. She wanted to call out to him and tell him he was not alone, but in an instant, Caleb had carried her past the prisoners.

Where was Juanita? And little Miguel? Slowly, painfully, she turned her head to the hills where the soldiers were spread out searching for survivors. One soldier was walking toward Juanita's hiding place. She prayed they were still safely hidden in the brush on the hillside. If Juanita could keep the baby quiet, they had a chance.

Caleb arrived at a makeshift tent made of canvas and dumped her on the ground. She tried to lift her body so she could keep watch over Juanita's hiding spot, but she was too weak. She fell back, panting. Her head ached and she was dizzy.

From inside the tent, she heard Caleb say, "Doc, I've got an Indian girl here for you to look at."

"She'll have to wait until I'm done with our own boys," was the response.

Casita floated in and out of darkness. Finally the doctor emerged. "What do we have here?" He checked her wounds, then called for water to clean her up. Jeremiah went running with a clay pot toward the river.

"She's hurt pretty bad," the doctor said. "I don't know if she'll make it. Maybe we should just leave her."

"Orders are to keep her as a hostage," Caleb said sourly.

"Then clean her up best you can."

"Can't someone else do it?" Caleb asked. "I want to get back to the fighting."

"The fighting's over. You just want to loot. I know what you boys are like," the doctor said. "Do as you're told."

Jeremiah returned with the water. With angry, jerking motions, Caleb swabbed away the blood with a filthy cloth. Casita might have told him no medicine man would use a dirty cloth to clean a wound, but what would be the point? He glared at Casita with eyes that hated her as much as she hated him.

I'm a hostage, Casita thought. They would try to use her to force her father to surrender. Like her mother, Casita would rather die than let that happen. She was too weak to escape, so what were her options? Maybe if she were lucky, she would die on the trail before they reached Texas.

"I've been counting the dead," Jeremiah said. "We killed twenty and took forty prisoner. But there weren't only old men, not braves. We're still a long way from home and those braves could be hiding anywhere. They could attack anytime and we wouldn't see 'em coming."

35

Caleb said bitterly, "They'd love nothing better than to scalp all of us."

He was wrong, of course. The Apache did not enjoy scalping their enemies; it was a necessary evil in war.

"With all these prisoners, it's going to be slow going," Jeremiah said.

His words gave Casita hope. An army like this could not pass unnoticed through the rough terrain between here and the Rio Grande. Her father was a great warrior with many friends. If he learned what had happened, he could lay a trap for the soldiers. And all their guns and ammunition wouldn't matter then. Casita's longing for revenge would only be satisfied when the soldiers were dead or dying.

All hope wasn't lost. Not yet.

Nde'

CHAPTER FOUR

N O SOONER HAD CALEB BANDAGED HER UP THAN AN OFFICER rode up, issuing orders.

"Get the prisoners ready to travel," he bellowed. "I want us on our way by noon. With luck, we'll be back at Fort Clark tomorrow night."

"Yes, sir, Captain Carter," Caleb said, saluting.

Before, she had only seen chaos when the soldiers had attacked—but now she saw how each soldier was part of a single animal obeying the commands of Captain Carter. As they rounded up the tribe's horses and secured the prisoners, their expertise dismayed her. With the soldiers' weapons and their training, her people had been easy to defeat.

A bitterness filled her mouth when she saw Indians among the soldiers. Their skin was a deep, dark brown and they didn't wear uniforms. Some had on battle headdresses. These must be the Seminole scouts who worked for the Army in

37

exchange for money, food, and land. Even her father admired their scouting skills and their fierceness in battle. But they had led the soldiers to the Ndé's hidden home. She thought she might hate them even more than the soldiers.

Caleb lifted her and dropped her hard on a straw-colored pony. He had meant to hurt her, so she refused to cry out. When her vision cleared, she recognized the pony as Jack's. She patted his neck. "Hello, Choya," she whispered. Her brother had named the pony for the cacti that grew like trees in the desert. His coat was sweaty but she pressed herself against his shoulder, grateful for his company.

A bugle sounded. The long train of scouts, followed by the officers, soldiers, mules, and finally the prisoners and their guards, fell into line. Casita was almost glad to leave. The teepees and the wickiups were still smoldering and the smell made her want to retch. The burial place of the dead was sacred to them, but not like this. She said a quick prayer to the spirits, reminding them it was not the Ndé's fault the dead had been tossed into the fire without respect. She asked Usen, the chief of all the spirits, to bless this place anyway.

Casita's eyes went to her favorite rock standing guard high above the valley. It could not burn. It would be there forever. But with each step away, Casita felt as though she would never return. Her ties to her childhood, family, band, and home were snapping, one by one.

If Jeremiah had counted correctly, then at least ten of the band might have escaped into the hills. She hoped Juanita and Miguel were among the safe ones. The soldiers seemed to have no appetite to stay and search. And she realized they were afraid. If the warriors returned, the soldiers would find themselves in the fight of their lives. Tired and low on ammunition, the soldiers were eager to get back to the safety of the Texas side of the Rio Grande.

The scouts led them out by a different route than the one they'd come in by. As they traveled, the soldiers had orders to stay quiet. Caleb and Jeremiah rode in front of her, speaking in whispers.

"What's wrong with you?" Caleb asked. "You look like we lost the battle."

"I've been listening to the officers," Jeremiah answered. "They're worried."

"About the Indians? We didn't lose a single man today," Caleb said. His gloating made Casita wish she had Jack's bow so she could shoot an arrow into his back.

Jeremiah leaned closer to Caleb. "What if the braves are just waiting to ambush us?"

"They're no match for us," Caleb said. Casita heard a trickle of fear in his voice.

Jeremiah glanced round to be sure they weren't overheard. "And we might have trouble from the Mexicans, too. We're not supposed to be on this side of the Rio Grande. They could take us prisoner and they'd be in the right."

Casita loved how frightened they were. But listening to them, she realized that the Ndé had been foolish to think the Army would respect anyone's laws, even their own. She prayed to Usen that a vicious counterattack would come. She kept watch on the horizon, but there wasn't any sign of her father's men.

The long ride was a blur as Casita's injuries took their toll. The plodding pace and the sun beating down on her bandaged back gave her a headache. The cruel sun baked the long line of riders and there was no breeze to relieve them. The dust kicked up by the horses settled on their riders. Casita was thirsty all the time. Her people knew better than to travel during the hottest part of the day, but the bluebellies insisted on traveling when the sun was highest. They didn't dare stop and rest. The smallest children kept falling asleep and tumbling off their horses. Captain Carter finally gave orders to tie them to their mounts.

It seemed like weeks had passed, but when Casita saw the moon rise, she realized it was still the same day. A day begun with joy and promise had ended in screams and tragedy.

The moon was a familiar friend, but tonight she wished for clouds. The moonlight helped the soldiers find their way and would alert them to an ambush. They were traveling on a narrow track by a deep ravine when Casita saw a figure floating next to her in the shadows of the moon. She shook her head to clear her vision, but the figure remained, a tall woman in buckskin who hovered above the ravine. She beckoned to Casita.

"Mother?" Casita whispered. Did Mother want Casita to come to her? If Casita leapt into the ravine, she would die. Was that what Mother wanted? At least she wouldn't be a prisoner, heading for a reservation. Casita wanted to honor her mother, but was it right to leave her brother? What if Father was coming to rescue them? Then she would have wasted her life. She hated herself for being unable to decide. It was a weakness. Mother had not hesitated when she had to choose.

The figure silently snapped her fingers. It was a gesture Casita knew well. She unwrapped the pony's reins from around her hands. She would do as her mother asked and leap. Caleb and Jeremiah were leading their horses in front of her, but if she were quick, they could do nothing to stop her. She took a deep breath.

A flash of light startled her. Caleb had pulled her mother's necklace from his pocket to take a closer look. The mirrored surface caught the moon and reflected it into the night. Her mother's spirit vanished. Instantly there was a ripple of noise as the soldiers ahead of them noticed the light. Rifles were brought to bear, and she could hear pistols being cocked up and down the line.

A scout came racing back on foot. "Put that away! Do you want to tell the Apache exactly where we are?" the Seminole accused in English. "If they attack here, half of us would be in the ravine before we could get a shot off."

His angry voice pulled Casita back, giving her a moment to think. She had been wrong. Her mother wasn't there for her; Mother had been lured by her necklace. The Ndé burned their dead with all their possessions so their spirits would be content. When Caleb had taken her mother's most prized possession, he had condemned her spirit to wander.

"I don't take orders from you." Caleb spat in the dirt at the Seminole's feet. The way Caleb looked at the scout told Casita he hated all Indians, not just her people. Even the ones who were on his side.

The Seminole's mouth tightened. Casita moved her hand to catch his eye. "What it is it, little one?" he asked softly in halting Apache.

"The necklace was my mother's," she whispered. "She died in the raid. May I hold it?"

His dark eyes looked kindly at her as he nodded. Turning to Caleb, he held out his hand. "Give it to me."

"You can't make me!" Next to him, Jeremiah whispered a warning to Caleb. Casita didn't blame him. The Seminole was older, heavier, and a battle-hardened fighter. Both boys together wouldn't stand a chance against him.

"Boy, don't make trouble for yourself over a stolen trinket," the Seminole warned. "Captain Carter'll cashier you out of the Army for giving our location away to the enemy."

Slowly Caleb dropped the necklace in the scout's palm, then pulled his hand back as if he were afraid to touch him.

The Seminole gave it to Casita. Solemnly, she thanked him. The pendant felt heavy in her hand. Rubbing her thumb across the stones, she knew what she had to do. Mother's spirit would not rest until it had the necklace. Biting her lip against the pain, she drew back her arm and managed to throw the necklace as far into the ravine as she could. Caleb lunged toward it, but Jeremiah held him back. "It's not worth dying for, Caleb," Jeremiah said.

42

Caleb turned his anger toward Casita, lifting a hand to hit her. The Seminole stopped the blow midair with his huge hand. "The Captain wants the prisoners in good condition," he said. He held Caleb's gaze until Caleb backed down.

"Are you crazy?" Jeremiah asked after the scout had returned to the front. "Seminole Jim is one of the toughest scouts there is."

"He's still an Indian once all's said and done," Caleb muttered, glaring at Casita. He had hated her kind before, but now his anger was directed squarely at her. Casita did not care. Her only thought was of her mother. Now she could rest.

As she closed her eyes she could almost feel her mother's hand soothing her brow, and then, just as blessedly, she felt her mother's presence fade away.

When next she woke, they had stopped at a small stream. Finally, a chance to rest and drink. Jeremiah let Casita dismount and sit against a rock. A low-voiced command came down the ranks to water the horses. Even the smallest Ndé child knew how vulnerable you were when your horse was drinking. The soldiers did, too. They posted guards at all the approaches to the waterhole. But nothing could ease their fears. Even the officers jumped at every rustle in the brush.

Casita prayed that every sound was her father's men sneaking up on them. Despite her hopes, she was still startled when she felt a tug at her leg. She gasped when she saw it was Jack.

"How did you get away?" she whispered.

"They are too tired to watch me," he answered just as quietly. "Where is Mother?"

He didn't know.

"She is dead," she finally managed to say. "They shot her."

Jack trembled as he tried not to cry. Mother would be proud of him; she had no patience with self-pity. After a long moment, he recovered. "We have to go."

Casita wanted to, but the throbbing in her shoulder told her otherwise. "I'm hurt. You must go without me."

"I cannot leave you alone—not after I let Mother die."

"You didn't let her die. You fought the soldier. You were brave," she protested. "Run as fast as you can. Find father and tell him what's happened. That is how you can save all of us." She was doing the right thing—she was sure of it—but sending Jack away was the hardest thing she had ever done. Without him, she had no family.

He gripped her hand tightly but did not say a word. "Please go," Casita urged. "If I'm with you, I'll slow you down."

She felt him start to tremble again. "Go, little brother," she repeated.

He stared at her for a long moment and then disappeared into the darkness.

All the Ndé were trained to be stealthy, but Jack was particularly good at disappearing. She prayed to Usen he would succeed. But at the same time, she felt utterly alone. How much more could she lose?

She listened intently but could only make out the groans

of the tired soldiers and the horses drinking their fill. But then she heard a yelp and a scuffle. A shot rang out, echoing around the huge boulders surrounding the watering hole. She cried out, then clamped her hand over her mouth. She must not show weakness even if her heart was breaking. Had Jack been caught? Was he dead?

She hardly dared to breathe. As the command came to remount, she saw Seminole Jim walking down the line of horses and men. He saw her and nodded. She beckoned him over. "I heard a shot," she said.

He answered her in Apache. "A boy tried to escape. We caught him."

"Is he . . . is he still alive?" she managed to ask.

He nodded. "But they've got him trussed up behind a soldier now. He won't be going anywhere."

"Thank you," she said, her voice trembling. Jack still lived. She knew he must be hurting. And he'd feel humiliated. Afraid. Angry. But the only thing that Casita felt was gratitude. She wasn't alone after all.

PART TWO

Nde'

Nde'

CHAPTER FIVE

Fort Clark, Texas

At DAWN, THEY DESCENDED INTO THE RIVER VALLEY. THIS WAS THE
Rio Grande, the great river marking the border between
Mexico and Texas. The scouts led them to a ford where the
river was shallow enough to cross. Casita listened to the fear
in the soldiers' voices and saw how their eyes raked the trees
and brush. If her father had found out about the raid, if he
could gather enough allies to attack, if he could reach them
in time—this would be the place for an ambush.

The exhausted soldiers hurried to get themselves and
the prisoners across the river. Seminole Jim went first, the
water reaching above his waist. But no matter how desperate,
the crossing of three hundred men and two hundred horses
still took time. The need for quiet made it even harder. One
soldier fell off his horse and nearly drowned.

"Tie all the prisoners to the horses," came the order from
Captain Carter. "We don't want to lose anyone."

The hours passed, and one by one, the soldiers climbed up the embankment on the Texas side of the river. By the time Casita crossed, she had lost hope. No silhouette of a scout had appeared on the ridge. No rustle in the underbrush betrayed a warrior's stealthy approach. No arrows pierced the throats of her captors.

As her pony lurched up the Texas side of the river, Casita slumped down and lay her cheek on Choya's damp neck. "We are lost," she whispered.

But so long as she and Jack were alive and together, there was hope. Casita had only one goal now. To survive.

Casita's head ached from the merciless sun. Her buckskin tunic was stiff with dried blood. Flies landed on her and she lacked the strength to wave them away. She knew she would fall off her pony if she hadn't been tied down. She let her eyes close and prayed to Usen that her suffering would be short.

A great shout rose up from the soldiers as Fort Clark came into view. Although the horses were as exhausted as the riders, their pace picked up as they neared home.

They passed a deep, wide pond surrounded by Spanish oak trees just below the fort. Water. She felt desperate for a swallow of cold water. The skin across her face felt tight and dry. Her eyes fixed on the spring, her body lurched forward. But the ropes tying her to Choya cut cruelly into her chest.

"Whoa! What are you doing?" Caleb was suddenly at her side, pulling her roughly onto the pony's back. "I brought you this far alive, didn't I?" He looked at her closely and then touched her face with the back of his hand. "You're hot. Captain Carter'll kill me if you die from fever on my watch." His breath smelled of tobacco and made her gag. He pulled out his canteen and dribbled water on her lips. "Wait to die until I get you to the infirmary. Then you won't be my problem anymore," Caleb said.

The long line of soldiers and prisoners started up the hill to the fort. The horses' hooves clattered as they broke into a trot across the wooden bridge and through a wide opening, flanked by a tall guard tower. A crowd of soldiers and women cheered when they saw the prisoners, a sure sign that the raid had been successful. Casita hated them all for it. How could people cheer for the massacre of her family? But then she remembered how she and Jack used to whoop when her father returned from a raid. Had her father left a trail of broken bodies and burned homesteads, too?

Leaving the others behind, Caleb led Choya across an enormous open square bordered on all sides by large buildings. He took them to a long white building set back from the others that lined the square. Caleb called to someone inside, "Get a doc! She's hurt bad!"

Casita swayed back and forth, her head dizzy. The surprise she felt at the urgency in his voice must have been reflected in her face, because Caleb muttered in her ear, "Don't think I care if you live or die, Apache. I'm just following orders."

A man in uniform came running down the steps. He lifted

Caleb's rough bandage, now soaked through with blood, to look at Casita's wounds. "Cut her off that horse," the doctor ordered.

"Yes, sir." Caleb's knife slid along the skin of her arm and she felt the tightness of the ropes fall away. She toppled to one side, but the doctor grabbed her before she hit the ground. As he carried her inside the building, a woman in a dark dress and a white apron appeared at Casita's side.

"Oh my!" the woman said. "She's only a little girl." She brushed away the hair from Casita's forehead and caught her breath when Casita winced. "I'm sorry, honey." They were the first gentle words Casita had heard since the raid. This unexpected kindness startled her, and Casita tried to get a better look at the woman.

"Watch her, Mrs. Smith," the doctor warned. "Even Apache children are dangerous."

"Heavens, Dr. Mallory, she's barely conscious."

"You've only just arrived in Texas, ma'am. These people are ruthless fighters."

"But she's a child!"

"I think this one might be the daughter of someone important." Caleb's voice came from behind Casita. "Her mother had a necklace with blue stones that was worth a pretty penny."

"I don't care if she's the Empress of China," Mrs. Smith said. "She needs our help."

"And she'll get it," Dr. Mallory said. "I know my duty.

But I'll watch her like a hawk. Mrs. Smith, you'll do the same if you want to continue helping in the hospital."

"Of course, Doctor."

Lying in the doctor's arms, Casita couldn't get a good view of the room, but she could tell it was big and full of light. Dr. Mallory brought her to the far corner and placed her on a bed.

"You're safe here," Mrs. Smith murmured. "Sleep."

Despite the brightness, Casita couldn't keep herself awake. Slowly her eyes closed and she surrendered to sleep.

❖

Casita woke to someone bathing her wounds with a wet cloth. If she didn't open her eyes, she could pretend it was her mother tending her wounds. Pretend that life was still the same. But a voice speaking English interrupted her pretty dream.

"Poor thing. Who would do this to a little girl?" Mrs. Smith's voice was as soothing as her hands. After a few minutes, she finished her work, but Casita didn't hear her moving away. Casita slowly opened one eye. The room was dimmer now. Her bed had been cordoned off with canvas screens. Mrs. Smith rested in a nearby chair, her eyes closed. A tendril of blond hair escaped from her cap and lay against her pale cheek. Casita had never seen skin so white. Suddenly, Mrs. Smith woke up, blinking her bright blue eyes. As blue as the sky stone in Mother's necklace.

"Hello, young lady. Welcome back!" Mrs. Smith said. "I know you don't understand me, but the doctor said you are going to be fine." Pointing to herself, Mrs. Smith said, "My name is Mollie Smith. What is yours?"

Casita was silent, not daring to reveal how much she understood.

Unconcerned, Mollie Smith said, "Never mind about your name for now. I'll be taking care of you. While you were asleep we cleaned you up. I would never have thought one little girl could be so dirty! We had to burn what you were wearing, but we have new clothes for you."

Casita's hand went to her neck. Her fingers touched thick bandages. Where was her father's necklace?

Beyond the screen they could hear two men talking. Casita recognized Captain Carter's voice.

"When can the girl travel? The colonel wants to ship the others out in a few days," Captain Carter said. "The sooner they are on the reservation at Fort Gibson, the better."

Casita knew all about the white men's reservations: the illness, the rotten food, the barren ground, and the liquor that made brave men foolish. It was no life for the Ndé. Her mother had died rather than go to one.

"She was badly hurt. She might not survive the trip to Oklahoma," Dr. Mallory said.

"Fine. What's one more dead Indian?" the captain demanded. "Just don't delay me."

"How despicable," Mollie muttered. She pushed herself

54

out of her chair—no doubt to scold the men beyond the screen. Casita felt a tiny spark of hope. This woman wanted to help. Casita reached out and grabbed her hand.

Startled, Mrs. Smith looked down. "What is it, my dear?"

"Help me! Please!" Casita whispered.

"You speak English?" Mrs. Smith said.

"I can't go to the reservation," Casita cried. "If you don't save me, I'll die."

Nde'

CHAPTER SIX

As the men spoke again, Casita put her finger to her lips to warn Mrs. Smith to be silent.

"We can't afford to wait for a sick girl," Captain Carter said. "The Apache have never dared to attack the fort, but we've dealt them a vicious blow. They might do anything if they think they can rescue their people."

"Don't worry, dear," Mrs. Smith said quietly. "I'll handle this." She pushed back the screen. Casita could just make out the doctor and Captain Carter.

"Mrs. Smith!" Captain Carter said, surprised. "Good afternoon."

"Please keep your voices down," she said. "My patient is trying to rest."

Captain Carter snorted. "*Your* patient, Mrs. Smith?"

The doctor said with a slight smile, "Mrs. Smith is a nurse."

"I met my husband at Gettysburg while he was recuperating," Mrs. Smith said. "He needed rest after that terrible battle, and so does this little girl." Both men glanced at Casita, then quickly looked away.

"Patient or not, she's a prisoner of war," Captain Carter said. "When will she be able to travel?"

"Soon," the doctor reassured Captain Carter.

"It may be some time," Mrs. Smith contradicted him.

"It'd best not be too long," Captain Carter said. "Or I'll take her anyway and damn the consequences." He turned on his heel and Casita heard his boots marching out of the infirmary.

"Doctor, may I speak with you?" Mrs. Smith drew the doctor away, out of earshot. Watching her go, Casita wondered if she could trust a white woman. Without her band, without allies, she was powerless to help herself and Jack.

Alone for the rest of the day, Casita had time to wonder about where she was. Her little space behind the screen offered hardly any information. There wasn't much to see: a thin bed, a chair, a small table, and a bucket to pee in. The acrid smell of whatever they used to clean the floors made her stomach churn. Beyond the screen, she could hear the doctor talking to his other patients. From what she could make out, they were soldiers from the raid grumbling about the Indian girl who was getting special treatment.

She was anxious to know about the world outside her

little space, but she had no way to see. Every few minutes, she heard the sound of a bugle, but she had no idea what it meant. Where was Jack? And what was going to happen to her? She remembered how Mother had taught her to tackle a big problem a little bit at a time. She and Jack had survived the raid. The next step was to keep them from the reservation. Her only weapons were her cleverness, her ability to speak English, and Mrs. Smith.

She was relieved when Mrs. Smith returned as promised.

"Hello, dear." Mrs. Smith made a show of checking behind the screens. "I wouldn't want anyone to overhear," she explained. "What is your name?"

Casita did not hesitate. She must make this woman a friend, and quickly. "I am called Casita."

"What a lovely name. What does it mean?"

"To my people it means 'girl of the small house.'"

"Do you have a last name?"

"My father is called Raul Castro."

"So Casita Castro. You can call me Mollie. How can you speak English so well?"

"My father taught me," Casita said, letting her voice tremble. To show weakness would be the way to get Mollie on her side. And she needed Mollie's help if she wanted to see Jack again.

"Is your father a prisoner?" Mollie asked.

Casita shook her head. "He was away when the soldiers came."

"What happened on the raid?" Mollie asked, leaning

forward with her elbows on the bed. "I have only just come to Fort Clark and I don't know what the soldiers have to do."

As Casita recounted the day, from the first rifle shot to her mother's body being tossed into their burning home, she felt as if she were at the edge of a campfire circle, listening to someone else tell the story. In her mind, she called it the Day of Screams. Surely this was how the day would be remembered if anyone in her band survived.

"I am so sorry," Mollie said, horrified. "That wasn't a fair fight at all, but a massacre of children and women."

Casita wasn't familiar with the word *massacre*, but she agreed that the raid had not been fair. On the other hand, who expected war to be fair? This Mollie Smith had odd ideas for someone who lived in an Army fort.

"But what happened to your brother?"

Casita answered, "I don't know. He tried to escape, but he was captured. I am afraid he might be hurt."

"He's not in the hospital—I would know if there were another child here. I can try to find out for you."

"But aren't you a soldier's wife?" Casita asked.

"I am, but I'm a Quaker and we believe in helping people, even our enemies."

"Can you keep me and Jack away from the reservation?"

"Why wouldn't you want to go to one?" Mollie asked. "They're supposed to be the solution to the Indian problem."

"That's a lie," Casita said boldly. "They choose land where nothing grows and there is no game for hunting. And the water is dirty. People get sick and die. Reservations are really prisons without bars. I know. I have heard it many times. My brother would die of shame there." She reached out to take Mollie's hand. "You've got to help us."

"I don't know what I can do. The Army won't listen to me."

"Because you are a woman?"

Mollie nodded.

"My people respect women. My mother was strong." Casita's gaze fixed on those odd blue eyes. "You are strong, too. I heard you speak to Captain Carter."

"Where I am from, women are equal to men. But that is not the way in the Army," Mollie said. "And there is only so much trouble I can make without getting my husband upset."

"Make trouble for us," Casita pleaded.

"First things first," Mollie said. "I'll go see what I can find out about your brother. I'll be back soon."

First things first. Mollie sounded like Mother. Casita let her head fall back on the soft pillow and stared at the ceiling. Mother would never ask a white woman for anything. If she were here, she would tell Casita to rely only upon herself. But Casita had no choice but to look to someone else. And she didn't have much time. As soon as she was healed, the doctor would send her away.

And what about Jack? He had not waited for help; he had tried to escape on his own. But that hadn't worked. The soldiers were too many and too strong. Had they hurt him when they caught him? Was he still alive? She couldn't lie here for another minute without knowing. She couldn't wait for Mollie. How hard could it be to find a group of Indian women and children in a military fort? He must be close by.

She threw back the covers and swung her legs onto the floor. Her bare feet touched the wooden planks and she swayed for a moment until the dizziness went away. She wore a soft cotton dress that went down to her feet. Casita guessed it belonged to Mollie. Her ankle was sore, but she could walk on it.

Peeking past the curtain, she saw the room beyond had only a few patients in beds. One patient had a visitor sitting with him, his back to her. The doctor was nowhere to be seen. Quickly, before she could think better of it, she crossed the room and slipped out the same door Captain Carter used. She found herself outside on a terrace filled with chairs for patients. No one was sitting there this late in the day. The sun was setting in a brilliant display of oranges and reds, the same as it did at home. The hospital was set back in a corner of the great square. It was like a miniature town. Everywhere she looked there were soldiers, drilling on horseback, marching on foot, lounging about, or playing games. Some, no doubt, were the ones who had murdered her people. How could she ever find Jack? The prisoners could be anywhere.

Casita watched a soldier march to a flagpole in front of her and start playing a battered bugle. A song without sweetness or melody. But it must have been some kind of signal, because the horsemen left the square. The marching men and the others headed to a long, low building. Even from where Casita stood she could smell meat cooking. Maybe this was a good time to look, while they were all eating . . . but before she could go into the square, she was grabbed from behind.

"Where do you think you're going?" Caleb's mouth was so close to her ear that she could feel his spittle on her skin. "A filthy Indian's not fit to be walking about free." He twisted her arm behind her and shoved her back inside. She cried out before she could stop herself.

Dr. Mallory spotted them and hurried over. "What are you doing, Caleb? You're supposed to be sitting with Major Jameson, not walking the prisoner."

"I was," Caleb said. "But then I saw her trying to leave and I caught her before she could get too far." He twisted her arm even further and the pain made Casita feel queasy. She would have tumbled if Caleb hadn't held her up.

"Good job, son," Dr. Mallory said. "I wouldn't want to have to explain to Carter what happened to his prisoner."

"She's a troublemaker," Caleb said. "I saw that on the ride home."

"She'll be gone soon. Put her in her bed. Mrs. Smith will be back in a moment and she can sit with her."

"But what if she tries again?"

"If she does, I'll hand her over to Carter, injured or not."

Caleb dragged Casita to her bed. "Stay there or I'll wallop

you next time," he warned. "I wish you knew English so I could tell you what I think of you."

When Mollie came around the screen, she was surprised to see Caleb. "What are you doing here, Caleb?"

"This Indian tried to escape, Mrs. Smith."

Mollie laughed. "She can hardly walk."

"Ma'am, you're too trusting. She's stronger than you think."

"I can take care of myself and the girl," Mollie said, still smiling. "I hear you are doing well with Dr. Mallory."

Caleb's back straightened and he glanced over to where his other patient lay. "I am. The doc says I have a knack with the injured patients."

"Good for you. And come back to me anytime you wish to continue your schooling," Mollie said warmly. "Your parents would have wanted it."

Caleb's pride was replaced by sadness. He backed out of sight. As soon as she was sure he was gone, Casita said, "He's a devil!"

"Casita! Don't be silly. Caleb is just a boy. He was fourteen when his family was killed. He's only sixteen or seventeen now."

"He threw my mother's body into the fire and stole her necklace."

"Caleb did that? He must have had orders. Even good people have to do bad things in war."

Casita shook her head. "He enjoyed it."

"Oh, I'm sure that's not true."

"He hates my people."

Mollie stroked Casita's hand. "He has cause, Casita. An Apache raider killed his father and brother and burned down his house."

"He was happy to do the same to my family."

"The only way to stop this awful war is for everyone to forgive each other."

"Forgive?" Casita wasn't familiar with the word.

"It means to learn to love your enemies. Quakers don't believe in war or violence."

Privately Casita thought Mollie's people, these Quakers, sounded weak. Sometimes vengeance was necessary. "War is not the way of Ndé either," Casita said after a moment. "We fight to survive."

"Enday?" Mollie asked, trying to pronounce the unfamiliar word.

"It is what we call ourselves. My people are the Cuelcahen Ndé—the people of the tall grass."

"I thought you were Apache?"

"We are Apache, too. There are many different bands who are Apache, but only my band is Cuelcahen Ndé."

"The Army may see you as enemies, but the Quakers believe there is a peaceful solution to the Indian problem. I do, too."

Without expecting much, Casita asked, "Is there a solution to my problem?"

"I have an idea that will keep both you and your brother here," Mollie said.

"Tell me, please," she said. Even if Mother would not approve, Mollie was their best hope.

"Not yet," Mollie said. "First I have to make sure I can do it. You'll have to trust me."

"I do trust you," Casita answered with a spark of hope.

Nde'

CHAPTER SEVEN

CASITA KNEW SHE WAS RUNNING OUT OF TIME, ALTHOUGH THE only way she could mark it was by the never-ending bugling. From sunrise to sunset, the Army seemed to have signals for every hour, reminding her that any day now, she and Jack would be shipped out. The only thing that stood between them and the reservation was Mollie's promise. Had Casita made a terrible mistake trusting this white woman?

It was three days after they met when Mollie came to check on the wound on the back of Casita's shoulders. "Does that hurt, my dear?"

Casita shook her head.

"You will always have the scars, but the pain will fade."

Casita fingered the healed wounds. Jack was the one who was supposed to have battle scars. Mollie had managed to find out that he was alive, but not much more. Casita had to believe that she would see him soon and they could compare whose scars were worse.

Dr. Mallory appeared from behind the screen. "How is she?" he asked. Mollie peeled back the bandages and he examined the wounds closely. "Very nice, Mrs. Smith. You've done a remarkable job."

"I hope I haven't healed her just so she can be carted away to a reservation," Mollie said.

"Best place for them." Dr. Mallory let out an impatient snort. "Besides, it's not for us to question our orders."

"*Your* orders," Mollie said sharply. "I'm not in the Army."

"You're an Army wife now," Dr. Mallory pointed out. "You had better get used to obeying orders without question. As your husband does." He paused and then said very pointedly, "Lieutenant Smith has a promising career in front of him."

Casita's eyes darted between the doctor and Mollie; she knew a threat when she heard one. "So if I don't toe the Army line, Charles will pay the price?" Mollie asked.

Casita feared that Mollie would never help her if doing so hurt Mollie's husband.

The doctor's voice softened. "Look, Mrs. Smith, I'm just trying to help. I know you are a Quaker and sympathetic to the Apache, but that attitude will only cause you grief here. We've all lost friends to these Indians' savagery. As he left for his rounds, he instructed, "Make sure she has extra bandages for the journey."

"Yes, sir." Mollie's voice was respectful but still defiant.

She peeked around the screen. "Wait until he hears that you are leaving here today with me!"

Casita sat up straight, wincing a little as her shoulder pulled against the bandage. "How?"

"You'll see in just a minute!"

"Mollie?" A tall man in a blue officer's uniform arrived. He had a slight limp. He wore the bushy sideburns that all the soldiers seemed to like. His face seemed naturally stern, but when he looked at Mollie he seemed to soften. Mollie quickly introduced them. "This is Lieutenant Smith, my husband." Lowering her voice, she added, "He knows you understand English." She was beaming, but Casita noticed how carefully she watched her husband.

"Hello, Casita," he said, extending his hand.

She hesitated. Casita had seen her father complete this ritual, but it was not for a child to do.

Mollie watched anxiously—she was nervous, Casita could see. "Shake his hand, Casita," she said.

"Only a chief shakes hands," Casita explained. "Not a girl child."

Charles was surprised, but he only said, "It's all right, Mollie," his hand back at his side.

"Hello, Lieutenant." Her tongue stumbled over the unfamiliar word.

"Call me Charles," he said. "My wife tells me you are almost well."

Casita nodded. This military man was not soft like his wife. She had better tread carefully.

"Do you hate us for raiding your village?" he asked abruptly.

"Charles!" Mollie cried, grabbing at his arm. "She's only a little girl."

He removed her hand from his elbow. "Mollie, I need to know this girl won't murder us in our beds." He turned his attention back to Casita. "The Apache women are as fierce as the men. I've seen what they can do." He smiled wryly. "In a way, it's a compliment. So, do you hate us?" he pressed.

Casita thought quickly. "Did you go on the raid?

"No," he answered. "I was injured during the war. Now I work for Captain Carter handling the paperwork to run the 4th Cavalry."

That made things easier, Casita thought. She wasn't sure she could live with one of the raiders who had massacred her village. As for the rest . . . what did he expect? Of course she hated them. But hate would only turn Charles against her.

"I am sad about my home. I miss my family." She spoke slowly and carefully. "But Mollie speaks of forgiveness. She has been very kind to me and I am grateful. I could not hate her."

"Don't you see, Charles, she can be taught!" Mollie said. "It is just as I always thought—the solution to the Indian problem is not war. It is love."

"What about the boy?" he asked. "Maybe you are right about the girl, but her brother would have grown up to be a warrior."

"Don't be ridiculous. He's even younger than Casita. We'll teach him our values," Mollie assured him.

69

"You don't know anything about him," Charles protested.

"My brother will be grateful, too," Casita said. "I promise you that."

Finally he said, "All right, but there are some conditions."

"Conditions?" Mollie said. "What conditions?"

"Captain Carter said they could stay and be our servants."

"Servants?" Mollie said indignantly.

"Not even you can get around this, Mollie," Charles said, holding up a hand. "There are rules for prisoners of war, which these two are, even though they are children. Officially, they have to be servants."

"But unofficially . . ." Mollie prompted, ". . . we can be a family."

"Maybe."

❖

The next morning Casita would finally see Jack. She dreaded what shape he'd be in, but she was glad they would finally be together. When Mollie arrived, it was the first time Casita had seen her without a cap. Her blond hair was drawn back in a tight knot and curly tendrils of hair bobbed about her ears.

"I have a new dress for you," Mollie said, handing Casita a small bundle. "You'll want to fit in at the fort."

Casita held the bundle and was unable to move. It wasn't Mollie's place to give Casita a new dress. That was for her mother.

"Casita?" Mollie nudged her. "Open it!"

She slowly unwrapped the paper to find a dark blue dress made of cotton. She stroked the fabric, softer than any buckskin could ever be.

Mollie watched nervously. "Do you like it?"

"I always wanted a dress like this," Casita said truthfully. She couldn't say that her mother had forbidden any Indaa clothes. But she really didn't have a choice; she didn't have anything else to wear.

Since Casita's shoulders were still sore, Mollie helped Casita out of the linen shift she wore. As Mollie started to fasten the buttons, Casita moved away.

"May I do it myself?" she asked.

Mollie looked hurt, but Casita knew she had to learn to fasten the dress by herself. She'd accept Mollie's clothes, but only on her own terms. It was the only way to keep faith with Mother.

Mollie watched as Casita figured out the buttons, her fingers mimicking the correct motions. Casita smiled to herself: Mollie would make a good mother someday. But she would never be Casita's.

"I don't have any shoes for you yet," Mollie said. "But we still have your boots." She pulled Casita's moccasins from under the bed. She held them up and looked at the upturned toes curiously. "I've never seen boots like these."

"They keep snakes away," Casita said.

"Oh," Mollie said. "Well, then you'll feel right at home at Fort Clark. I'm always finding snakes in my yard."

71

Casita stood up. The dress fell below her ankles, almost hiding the moccasins her mother had made for her.

"We're ready, Charles!" Mollie pushed the screen back.

Charles smiled at Casita. "You look very pretty."

"Doesn't she?" Mollie asked.

Casita wiggled her toes in the familiar moccasins. What the Smiths really meant was that Casita looked white. She would wear their dresses and do whatever was needed to fit in, but she must never forget that no matter how she dressed she was still Ndé.

"Hello, Lieutenant Smith," Casita said.

"You should call him Charles," Mollie said.

"I am your servant. Shouldn't I call you Lieutenant Smith?"

"Nonsense," Mollie began.

"No, Mollie, she's right," Charles interjected. "In private, you may call us Charles and Mollie. But around others, call us Lieutenant Smith and Mrs. Smith."

"Is that too hard to remember?" Mollie asked.

Casita shrugged, noticing the strange way the cloth dress constricted her chest. She was afraid it would rip if she took too deep a breath. The cloth was not as strong as buckskin. Maybe Mother had been right when she said the old ways were best.

"At home we have different names for people. My aunt is Alta around the fire, but when we ask her for spiritual advice, she is a medicine woman we call Altagracia. It is more respectful."

Charles stared. "Perhaps their ways aren't so savage after all," he said to Mollie.

"Can we go to Jack now?" Casita asked.

"I'll fetch him." Charles spoke too loudly, his voice echoing in the small space. "You two wait at home."

"Don't be silly," Mollie said, playfully hitting his arm. "We'll go together."

"I'd rather bring him to the house," Charles said, not meeting Mollie's gaze.

"Why can't we all go to get him?" Mollie demanded.

"The conditions aren't really suitable for a lady."

Mollie's blue eyes turned the color of gun steel. "Take us to him. We will see for ourselves."

Surrendering, Charles led the way outside, Casita following, quick on their heels. What had the US Army done to her little brother?

Nde'

CHAPTER EIGHT

CASITA HESITATED ON THE HOSPITAL STEPS. A COMPANY OF SOLDIERS marched by, rifles held at their shoulders. One turned his head to scowl at her. He wasn't fooled by this new dress. He knew an Apache girl hiding in plain sight when he saw one. She straightened her back and set off after Mollie and Charles with as much confidence as she could find in herself.

They went past a long building that was apparently only used to house horses. She counted twenty horses, then realized that this building was the first of several just like it. How many horses did they have?

Charles threaded a path through the stables to a large canvas tent. Its flaps were tied shut. A solitary guard sat outside, dozing with a rifle propped against his leg, until he heard their footsteps. He jumped to his feet and saluted Charles. Mollie pushed past the guard and began untying the tent flaps.

"Ma'am, you can't do that!" the soldier protested. He was young, and despite his weapon, Casita guessed he had never seen battle. He certainly did not know how to handle Mollie Smith.

"Private, it's all right," Charles reassured him. "Captain Carter has given us permission to bring out one of your prisoners."

The private looked beyond Charles and noticed Casita. "What's that Indian doing here?" His rifle was already pointing at her.

"She is with us," Mollie said. "Now kindly put that gun down." She finally managed to undo the tent ties.

Charles nodded at the guard and the gun was lowered. Mollie grabbed Casita's hand and they went inside. Before their eyes adjusted to the dark, the smell hit them like a blow.

"Where are the sanitary facilities?" Mollie demanded, covering her mouth and nose with a handkerchief.

"We give 'em buckets," the soldier said helpfully.

Mollie started to argue with Charles and the guard. Casita couldn't wait a moment longer to find her brother, but it was hard to make out the dozen or so children huddled inside. Casita went up to each child, each as familiar to her as Jack was. Each miserable face stabbed at her heart. Somehow when she was plotting to save Jack, she had managed to forget the suffering of these children. They were all going to the reservation while she and Jack would be saved. She wanted to take each one with her, but she knew it was impossible. She could only rescue her brother, if only she could find him.

A low groan caught her attention. In the far corner, a body lay on the ground. She moved closer. It was a boy on his side, his back to her. His long ponytail was crusted with dried mud. Casita hurried over, but then stopped short. It was Jack, she was sure of it. But he was so still. She hesitated, afraid of what she might find. She touched his shoulder and felt him move. He was still alive. "Jack?" she whispered. "It's Casita. I'm here." She tried to turn him over on his back, but his body clenched into a ball.

"Is that him?" Mollie called from the tent entrance.

"Yes," Casita said. "Wait there, please." Then, "Brother, it's me," she whispered in their language. "I've come for you." Slowly his body relaxed and she was able to turn him on his back. Jack's face was bloody and bruised and he was only able to open one eye. The other was swollen shut. Casita tried hard not to let her anger show.

"Sister?" he whispered.

"I'm here to rescue you."

His cut lip twisted into a smile. "That's not right," he said. "I'm supposed to save you."

She clapped her hand over her mouth to keep a sob of relief inside. "We can argue about it later," she promised. "I'm here to take you with me. We can be together."

"They're going to take us to the reservation at Fort Gibson," he said, his voice raspy as though he had not used it in days.

"We're not going."

"But . . . how?"

"I don't have time to tell you now. Just follow my lead. Can you stand?"

He lifted his wrists. He wore manacles attached to a tent pole. A wave of hate swamped Casita and she couldn't speak. Fortunately, Mollie couldn't keep quiet when she saw the chains. She rushed over, followed by Charles and the guard. "You've chained a little boy?"

Charles put his hand on her forearm. "Mollie, please, calm down."

"Ma'am, the boy tried to escape," the guard said. "Twice."

"Wouldn't you try to escape this?" Mollie asked.

Looking straight ahead, the guard said, "My orders are to keep these kids locked up."

"I'm going to have a word with Captain Carter about this," Mollie promised. "Now free the boy. He's coming with us."

Glancing at Charles, the guard said, "Sir, are you sure? He's a slippery one. And no offense, but you can't run very fast."

Charles grimaced. "Just unlock the chains," he ordered.

The guard brought out a key and the handcuffs fell off Jack's wrists.

Mollie's eyes went from Jack's bloody face to the bruises all over his body. "Casita, bring him out when you're ready," she said tactfully. She drew Charles and the private back outside, where no doubt she would have something to say about Jack's injuries.

Let her rant, Casita thought, as she helped Jack to his feet.

"Where are we going?" he asked, pressing his arm against his ribs as though they pained him.

"With them." She pointed to the Smiths.

He shook his head, puzzled. "They are Indaa."

"They're helping us," she answered.

"What about the others?"

"They'll be sent to the reservation," Casita said matter-of-factly, although her heart was breaking.

Jack straightened up and broke free of her. "Then I shall go to the reservation too."

"Brother, they will have their mothers to protect them. We are alone." Casita wanted to shake him. It had been hard enough to save the two of them. Jack could ruin everything if he didn't agree. "Listen to me, Brother. Mother died rather than go to the reservation."

"I'm a Ndé warrior. I'd rather die than hide with the pale faces," Jack said, examining the raw patches on his wrists from the manacles.

Leaning in close to his ear, she whispered harshly. "Think of Father. What did he tell us was the first thing the Cuelcahen Ndé must always do?"

Jack bowed his head. "Stay alive," he muttered.

"Our best chance is to stay here. Will you do as I ask?"

He thought long enough to worry her, but finally he nodded.

Casita led him outside to Mollie and Charles. "This is my brother, Jack."

While Mollie greeted Jack, Charles stared. Streaked with

blood and the river mud he had used as his war paint, Jack looked wild and fierce.

"You can't go walking about like that," Charles said. He unbuttoned his coat and tried to drape it around Jack's shoulder, but Jack ducked away like he'd been struck.

"Jack! He is a friend," Casita warned in their language. She picked up the coat and placed it across his shoulders.

Charles drew Mollie toward him and said, "For God's sake, Mollie, he's a savage. Are you sure?"

"Yes," she insisted. "More now than ever. We have to make up for the cruelty he suffered."

"What if he decides on revenge before we can do that?"

"He won't."

Casita was glad to see Mollie defend Jack, but she was afraid Charles might change his mind. She was determined to make sure that didn't happen.

As they left the tent, one of the other children called Jack's name. Casita pulled him away. "Don't look back. It will be easier."

Nde'

CHAPTER NINE

As Casita and Jack trailed behind the Smiths, the soldiers drilling in the parade ground stared. Casita tried to look small and harmless, but she noticed how Jack and Mollie straightened their backs and walked as though they had something to prove. Just a few minutes before, Jack had been chained to a post. But now he wore Charles's coat like it was his own, walking as if he were about to go into battle, his long tail of hair swinging as a challenge.

"You look like a warrior," she whispered.

"I am a warrior," he answered. "Didn't I fight the soldiers?"

"We cannot give them reason to be afraid of us," she warned. "You must act more like a mouse and not a mountain lion."

"The mountain lion can only hide for so long before he attacks," he told her.

They passed a large building that Charles told them was

the mess hall, where the soldiers without families ate. It was hard for Casita to imagine all these men without families. Among the Ndé, you always had family.

A dozen soldiers sat on the steps waiting to eat, including Caleb and Jeremiah. Jeremiah saw them first and elbowed Caleb's side. Caleb leapt to his feet and blocked Mollie's way.

"Mrs. Smith," he cried. "Why is she out of the hospital? And the boy? He's a prisoner."

"These children are coming to live in our home and be part of our family." Mollie spoke loudly so everyone could hear.

Casita saw Charles's reaction to Mollie's bold words. "As servants," he was quick to add.

There was an uneasy murmur among the soldiers, but only Caleb was furious enough to say what they were thinking.

"They're Apache!" he bellowed. "They'll murder you like they did my family. And then they'll let their tribe into the fort to kill the rest of us!"

"Caleb, they're children and will do no such thing," Mollie protested.

Next to her, Jack tensed.

"Brother, no!" Casita whispered fiercely.

Jeremiah tugged on Caleb's arm, but Caleb pushed him away. "I didn't go on that god-forsaken raid," he growled, "just so you could treat our prisoners like family." He moved closer, lowering his voice. "We risk our lives every day to protect you against the likes of them, and then you just take them in? It's wrong."

81

"We've taken their lands and killed their mother," Mollie answered defiantly. "So yes, I'm giving them a home." She looked at her husband and pleaded, "Charles. Do something."

Casita thought Charles agreed more with Caleb than with Mollie, but he was loyal to his wife. "Son, you are out of line," Charles said. To Jeremiah he said, "Get him out of here until he calms down. That's an order unless you'd both like to pull sink duty."

Apparently the threat of sink duty was a real one because Jeremiah hauled Caleb inside the mess hall.

Hurriedly, Charles took Mollie's arm. "That's just a taste of what we'll face," he warned.

Mollie patted his arm. "We'll meet it together."

"Who was that?" Jack asked Casita.

"No one important," Casita lied.

"He was on the raid, wasn't he?"

"Forget him. We can't have any fights. Charles is already worried about you. We have to act like the children they want us to be."

"We're Ndé," he answered, as though that settled the question.

Ahead of them, Charles was arguing with Mollie. And Casita was arguing with Jack. How could this plan possibly work?

Charles brought them to a row of identical stone houses facing the parade grounds. He called it "Officer's Row." Each house had a small wooden porch. In front there was a tiny area of scuffed dirt surrounded by a low fence. He kept going until they reached the last one.

"Your new home," Mollie said.

An Indaa house. With a stone foundation and doors and windows. If they lived there, they would never wander again. Casita would have given anything to have her wickiup back. Or to build a new one. Anything rather than trap herself inside a building that didn't move.

Mollie expected her to say something. Anything. Casita touched the fence, which didn't reach past her knee. "The animals you keep here must be very small."

"Animals?" Mollie said.

Casita tapped the fence.

Charles laughed. "That's not for animals. The fence is a marker to show where our yard begins and ends."

Jack and Casita exchanged knowing glances. What Mother had told them was true: even amongst themselves the Indaa were greedy and jealous of each other's property.

"Don't your people have fences?" Charles asked.

"Only to keep the horses in," Casita said. "But we live on the land, taking only what we need. We would never try to say, 'This piece is mine.' The land belongs to everyone."

"Well, this house is mine," Charles said, exasperated. "Mollie, why don't you show them around?" He pushed past Mollie and went inside.

"Charles!" But he didn't look back. "I know it must seem strange to you." Mollie smiled nervously. "It was strange to me when I first came. You will get used to it." She opened the door and gestured for them to come in.

Casita and Jack did not move at first. They had never entered a white man's house.

Mollie waited patiently. "Take your time," she said.

Jack eyed the doorway as though it was a trap. "I'll stay outside," he told Casita.

"We have to go in," Casita whispered. "We live here now."

"We could never live here."

On the parade ground behind them, a company of men on horseback trotted down to the end of the field in pairs. A bugle sounded, and the first ten pairs galloped forward. Then the pairs split down the middle, one column wheeling right, the other left. Then the next ten came. Casita could tell that they had practiced this often. She had seen this maneuver before. It was exactly the way the soldiers had attacked El Remolino. She looked away, back at Mollie's house. It was their only refuge now.

"I'm going in," she said. With a deep breath, she crossed the threshold. There. It was done. She looked at Jack. "I dare you to come in."

Jack strode forward, pushing past her into the room.

Both of them stopped, eyes wide. They stood in a long room with windows on the porch side and a fireplace at the other end. Casita took in every detail. From inside it seemed even bigger than it had from the outside. And so much larger than their wickiup. The walls were made of a hard white

84

plaster. The floor was not dirt, but wood. No wonder the Indaa cared so much about owning land. They built homes that were permanent. By building such a house, the white man was saying, *This is where I stay.*

Charles had disappeared. He must have left by the far door. Casita didn't blame him. Beginnings were never easy.

"This is the parlor," Mollie said. "This is where I sit and sew or read." She pointed to a sofa with soft-looking pillows. It looked functional enough, but why would anyone sit inside this airless room when they could be outside?

Casita moved about the room, looking for anything to reassure herself. Anything familiar. A table covered with a white cloth was in the center of the room. How did Mollie keep it so clean? There were pictures on the wall. Casita liked that. She would love to have a place to show her drawings instead of painting on baking stones or on the walls of cliffs. There was one picture of a house that interested her. It was made with thread. She reached out to touch it.

"Go ahead, Casita," Mollie encouraged. "It's needlepoint. The words say 'Home Sweet Home.'"

"But it isn't this house, is it?" Casita asked.

A shadow crossed Mollie's face. "No. It's the house where I grew up. This house is too new. It's not a home yet, but it will be."

Home for Casita was a round tent made of branches and skins. She glanced at Jack, who stood in the center of the room. In his dirty leather breeches and with Charles's coat hanging around him, Casita thought he looked like a wild animal trapped in a strange cage. He would never fit in. Neither of them would.

"Let me show you the kitchen," Mollie said, moving to the far door.

They followed, but Jack's attention was caught by a framed picture on the mantle. "Sister, look."

Casita picked it up. It was a likeness of Mollie and Charles. Mollie wore a light dress and Charles wore his military uniform. But the picture had no colors, only greys and browns. Mollie's bright blue eyes looked black.

"It's a photograph from our wedding," Mollie said, coming up behind them.

Casita had heard of photographs, but she hadn't seen one before. She could never capture a likeness like this. She turned it over, almost expecting to see their backs—the image looked so real.

"Are their souls trapped inside?" Jack asked. Casita translated for Mollie's sake.

Mollie burst out laughing. "It's just a picture. It doesn't take anything from us. In fact, we treasure it because it reminds us of a special day."

"Don't let anyone take it away," Casita said to Mollie. "Just in case your souls are there."

"I promise, we'll be very careful with it." Mollie gently placed the framed picture back on the fireplace. "But now, the kitchen."

Before they followed, Jack turned the photograph facedown on the mantle. "We don't want the gods to be offended," he said.

Casita set the photograph back to its proper position. "We have to live like them."

"They're asking for trouble," Jack warned.

As Casita led the way into the next room, she murmured to herself, "We're in trouble in more ways than one."

Mollie waited in a dingy room with a tiny window and a small iron stove. Casita understood this was, unlike the parlor, a room that was for preparing food. But the room stank of smoke and lye. A pot on the stove reeked of sour meat. Neither Jack nor Casita could keep their noses from twitching.

"You cook inside the house?" Casita asked.

Mollie laughed. "Of course. Where else would we cook?"

"Outside."

"What about in the winter?" Mollie asked.

"Always outside." To Casita's mind the reasons were obvious: less chance of fire and the smoke had somewhere to go.

"Father won't have time to find us," Jack muttered. "We will have died by fire."

For an instant, Casita's mind replaced the iron stove with their wickiup, aflame. Mother hadn't died by fire, but her body had been destroyed by one.

Mollie seemed disappointed in their reaction. But she was

determined to be cheerful. She showed them sacks of rice and corn in a larder, but Casita worried that Mollie didn't seem to notice the traces of mice. And Casita didn't understand how food got into the cans that lined the shelf. The Ndé grew, gathered, or hunted everything they ate.

Returning to the kitchen, Mollie pointed to a narrow stairway in the corner. "Our room is upstairs." Jack held back; he didn't like heights. Casita agreed. The stairs looked rickety and she worried they wouldn't hold their weight.

"Do we have to go up?" Casita asked.

"Not if you don't want to," Mollie answered, puzzled.

Finally Mollie showed them a small room off the kitchen. Inside were two pallets of straw with blankets heaped on top and two wooden crates.

"This is your room," Mollie said. "It's not much, but it is the best we can do for now."

"It's very nice," Casita said. She was glad that she and Jack would be together. Until this week, she could not remember a time she had not slept in the same space with him. His snores were soothing, and she had missed them in the hospital.

Jack scanned the room, measuring the narrow window, as if to make sure he could escape. How was she going to keep him from running?

Charles appeared in the doorway. "I've filled some buckets with water from the tank so Jack can get cleaned up." He held up a scrub brush and a tin of soap.

Jack shook his head and backed away.

"Nothing to scare a little boy like a bath!" Charles said with a grin. "Does Jack speak English?" he asked Casita.

"He doesn't speak much, but he understands more."

"I'm a good teacher," Mollie reassured them. "We'll do lessons until you both can read and write."

Casita translated. In English, Jack said slowly, "No school. I go outside."

Charles burst out laughing. "A young man after my own heart. I didn't like school either."

"Jack will do whatever you want him to," Casita said. "And so will I."

Nde'

CHAPTER TEN

Mollie and Casita sat in the kitchen listening to Jack's howls as Charles dumped bucket after bucket of water on him. They couldn't help but giggle.

"Poor Charles," Mollie said.

"Poor Jack," Casita replied.

"I suppose Jack has never had a bath before."

"We bathed every day in the river," Casita said. "Being clean is very important to us."

"To me, too," Mollie agreed. "I wish the soldiers around here agreed with us." She pinched her nostrils with her fingers.

For the first time since they had come into the house, they shared a smile. Mollie seemed to relax. Now Casita could see that she was as nervous as they were. But they both had reasons to make this arrangement work. Casita needed to survive and Mollie wanted to prove her point about Indians.

Once Jack was clean, Mollie presented him with new clothes. Jack was not pleased. He complained that the pants were uncomfortable until Charles informed him that he was wearing them backwards.

Charles tried to help him with the buttons on his new shirt. Jack shook his head, only allowing Casita to teach him. "How do you know how to do this?" he asked. "Mother never let us have clothes like these."

"Mollie taught me." In a low voice, she added, "Stop fighting with Charles or he'll send us away."

"I wish they would," he muttered.

Before Casita could argue with him, Mollie called them to dinner. They sat at the table in the parlor, afraid to touch the white tablecloth. Mollie explained all the utensils: a plate, a fork, and a knife.

"I know knives," Jack said.

Mollie served them the meat from the pot that they had seen in the kitchen. It was salty and Casita found it worrying that she could not identify the animal. There were beans, but they had been cooked so long they were mushy. Casita quickly mastered the fork, but Jack preferred to spear his food with the tip of his knife. He ate exactly like their father, quick with small bites.

"We'll starve," Jack whispered.

"Eat," she ordered. But she could not help but think of roasted agave hearts. Or corn cooked up with wild onions. Her mouth watered, remembering her mother's baked mescal cakes.

91

Mollie watched anxiously. "I'm afraid I'm not a very good cook."

"Of course you are," Charles said loyally.

Their stomachs weren't happy, but Jack and Casita cleaned their plates. "You like it," Mollie said, surprised and pleased.

"No," Jack said.

"It is new to us," Casita said. "We will learn to like it."

After dinner, Charles suggested they go outside and watch the evening Retreat Parade. Jack was eager to leave the stuffy house, and was first at the door. Charles followed close behind.

"He is afraid Jack will run away," Mollie confided.

Casita was, too, but she needed to comfort Mollie. "We have no place to run to."

Charles explained that the Retreat Parade happened every evening. Mollie laughed and said that all the days were alike at Fort Clark except Sunday.

They sat on a bench on the porch. The sun was just setting, bathing the full complement of soldiers in a reddish light. It was eerily silent. The soldiers stood at attention while the officers inspected the ranks. A band started playing a loud, brassy song as they marched down the field. When they passed the house, Casita saw that they had drums and flutes and some instruments she didn't recognize. When they had finished playing, the flag was lowered.

Casita thought the ceremony was over then, but the band started playing again. This time the soldiers marched in time and in perfect step all the way around the square.

Their discipline was frightening. No wonder the Army was so successful; the real question was how did the Ndé win any battles at all? *They could step on us like blades of grass under their boots*, Casita thought. Jack didn't say anything, but he edged closer to Casita on the bench. Finally the ceremony ended, and the soldiers were dismissed with a final bugle call.

"We live by the bugle," Mollie said. "Tomorrow morning you'll hear 'Reveille' when the sun rises and the men are supposed to wake up. Then 'Assembly,' when all the men will gather for roll call. 'Fatigue Call' is when work is assigned. 'Mess Call' when it is time to eat . . . 'Drills,' 'Stable Call' . . . all day long until it's dark. Then they play 'Taps' so we know it's time for bed."

Jack understood the gist of what she was saying and thought it was funny. Casita shook her head in warning.

Charles spoke sharply. "What's so funny?"

"That you don't know when to go to bed unless you hear a song," Casita said.

Mollie laughed and Charles looked annoyed. "There are hundreds of people in this fort, brought here for a common goal," he said. "The bugling keeps us on the same time. Discipline is the secret of the Army's success. You will soon get used to it."

A common goal? Casita knew the real reason Fort Clark was there—to fight the Indians. If the bugling was part of that, she decided she did not like it.

Charles asked Jack if he wanted to see more of the base. They set off together. They made a strange pair: the tall cavalry soldier in his uniform and the fierce Lipan Apache boy whose ponytail swung so defiantly. How could these two ever come together?

"Let's go inside," Mollie said. They sat on the sofa in the parlor. "Now we can talk."

"Won't there be a fire?"

"A fire?" Mollie repeated.

"At home everyone gathers after dinner around the fire. We tell stories into the night."

"I like that," Mollie said. "But that sounds like something families do, not the Army. Charles has always been a military man and he tells me the military is like a brotherhood. But it's not the same as having a real family—especially for me."

"Is that why you wanted us?" Casita asked. She had been so intent on keeping herself and Jack safe, she hadn't given much thought to what Mollie needed.

"I wanted to help," Mollie assured her. "But maybe I wanted company, too. I'm by myself all the time. The other officers' wives don't like my Quaker ideas."

"The Ndé live in large groups," Casita said. "We do everything together. We're hardly ever alone. We even sleep in the same room. My mother knew that sometimes it was hard for me." Casita's throat closed. The last time she had talked with her mother, she had discovered that her mother knew all about her private place.

Mollie took Casita's hand. "Tell me about her."

"She knew I needed to be by myself sometimes."

94

"She sounds wise. I'll make sure you have some time alone, too."

Mollie meant well, but what would Casita's real mother say about wearing this strange dress and sitting in an Indaa house? Would Father think she was clever to have found a safe place or a traitor for staying with the enemy? Especially when the others were headed to a reservation. She wished she could talk to them and ask them. But Casita had to be strong and push any doubts away.

❖

Before they went to sleep, Mollie showed them the privy behind the house. She opened the door so they could see the bench with a hole in the middle. She was too embarrassed to say what it was for, but its purpose was obvious. The smell was awful and Jack refused to go inside.

"How can they live like this?" Jack asked Casita in their own language.

"The Indaa like to close themselves in. They don't live out in the air like we do." To Mollie, she asked, "How does it get cleaned out?"

"The soldiers are assigned chores each week. This is 'sink duty.'"

Now she knew why Caleb had backed down so quickly when Charles had threatened him with sink duty.

The bugler played a long, mournful tune. Mollie said, "That is 'Taps.'"

At the door to their narrow room, Mollie seemed reluctant to leave them. "Will you be comfortable?" she asked.

"It is good," Casita assured her, sitting gingerly on the bed. She felt the straw poking through the sheets.

"Here are sleeping clothes." Mollie gave them linen shifts to wear to bed. On the table between the beds she placed a lantern turned down to a dull glow. "Your first night in a strange house, you might want a light. Good night, my dears." She closed the door behind her.

"How odd these Indaa are—they have special clothes to sleep in," Casita said.

She expected Jack to start complaining again, but he didn't say a word.

She let the silence grow until finally he burst out, "Sister, we shouldn't be here. We should run away."

"You already tried to escape and you were beaten." She would do anything to keep him from being hurt again.

"They won't be guarding us now."

"Where would we go? We have no horses, no supplies."

"The caves—" Jack started. The Ndé hid supplies in secret caves in the mountains in case of emergencies.

"Are all across the great river. We'd never reach them. Right now, Charles and Mollie trust us. If we run, they never will again. My plan is better."

"But you just want us to behave and wait," he complained.

"For now," she said. "It's the only way we can ever get home again."

After a long silence, Jack said, "But we have no home. It was burnt to the ground."

"Home is where our band is. You and I are the band for now."

"Do you think Father will look for us?" Jack asked.

Casita stared at the cracks in the adobe ceiling. "If he can. He has a better chance finding us here than all the way in Oklahoma."

"I won't become Indaa, though," he said.

"You don't have to. Just pretend. That is what I am doing."

"Are you pretending with Mollie?" He made it an accusation. "You seem to like her."

"Mollie will never replace Mother," Casita promised.

Casita could hear Jack toss from side to side. She could hear his soft moans.

"Are you hurting?" she asked.

"It's not bad."

She smiled in the darkness, remembering how proud Jack was of his ability to withstand pain. He could burn sage on his arm longer than any of the other boys.

After a while, he asked, "Are your wounds healed?"

She touched the scar on the back of her head. "Mostly."

"What happened to you . . . and to Mother?"

Casita remembered Jack had been unconscious in those final moments. "I don't remember very well. Mother was shot but she stood over me trying to protect me. Then I felt a terrible blow to my shoulders, then my head. After that it was only darkness."

"Are you sure Mother's dead?"

"I'm sure. I saw her body." *And her spirit*, Casita thought.

She heard an odd sound coming from the other pallet and realized her brave and reckless brother was trying to muffle the sound of his sobbing. She climbed out of bed to sit next to him. Rubbing his back in small circles the way her mother used to, Casita tried to stop his crying and comfort him.

"Brother, she showed no fear," she whispered.

"I failed her."

"You did not fail her!" Casita said. "She knew you fought the soldier. You hurt him badly."

"I couldn't save her."

"There were too many. No one could save her. And she chose to die protecting me rather than be taken prisoner. She died with honor."

"Was she buried with honor?" he asked, suddenly fierce. "Where is her body?"

The vision of mother's long hair hanging down as her body was tossed into the fire flashed into Casita's mind. "The soldiers burned it."

"I was afraid . . ." Jack's voice trailed off. She knew what he meant. He had feared that their mother's body had been left out for scavengers. "But there were no prayers. We didn't do any of the things we're supposed to do." She wanted to take him in her arms and hold him, but he would be deeply

98

offended if she did that. She had to help him be strong.

"Her spirit knows the truth. In such a battle, she would not expect us to stop and mourn," Casita said, tears running down her cheeks.

"We should do something," Jack insisted.

"I prayed for her. What else can we do? We are alone. There is no one to help us do the rites." They couldn't bury her in a sacred place. They had no drummers for the dance. Casita didn't know the funeral songs; that was something she would have learned only after her Changing Woman ceremony. Closing her eyes, she could almost feel her mother's clever fingers twisting her untidy hair into a neat plait. That was it. And she knew where to find a sharp knife. "Brother, there is one thing we can do."

Jack sat up in bed. "What?"

"Come with me," she said. She opened the door and peered out. Hearing nothing, she went into the kitchen, holding the lantern high so she could see. Casita felt uneasy, as though she were trespassing in a foreign land filled with strange metal objects; she was certain Jack did, too. She started searching the drawers until she found what she was looking for. She held up the sharp knife, the blade glinting in the light of the lantern. "It's not much, but Mother's spirit will know we tried."

Jack nodded, understanding now. "Yes. Do it." He turned his back to her.

"You are sure?" she asked.

His long tail of hair bobbed as he nodded. She held the ponytail, still slightly damp from the washing earlier, against the blade. She took a deep breath and, with a quick motion, cut off his hair at the nape of his neck.

There was nothing more precious to the Ndé than their long hair. Cutting it showed their grief and proper honor to their mother.

"Now me," Casita said, gathering her long hair in a bunch by her neck. Jack stood behind her, holding the knife to her neck, ready to cut, when a shriek filled the kitchen.

"Jack!" Mollie screamed.

Charles, in his nightshirt, came charging down the stairs, his rifle pointed at Jack's chest. "Drop the knife!" he ordered.

Nde'

CHAPTER ELEVEN

THE SUN WAS JUST BEGINNING TO STREAM IN THE TINY WINDOW. Casita propped herself on her uninjured shoulder to look down at Jack, still sleeping, on the floor. He looked so odd without his long ponytail.

She thought about the scene the night before. Once Mollie had understood what Jack and Casita were doing, she tried to convince Charles to put down his rifle.

"He has a knife to his sister's throat," Charles protested. "How do we know that he won't hurt her? Mollie, really . . . Are you sure this will work?"

"Charles, this is the way they mourn," Mollie insisted. "It will work if we are tolerant while the children get used to their new lives. They've suffered so much."

Slowly Charles lowered his rifle, and without speaking, turned and lumbered up the stairs. Mollie watched him. "You two are not the only ones who must get used to something new," she said. "Now, Casita, we need scissors if we're going to cut your hair." She hurried out of the room and returned with a sharp tool with two blades. With a few movements of the blades, Casita's hair fell to the floor with the slightest swishing noise. Casita touched her bare neck with a trembling hand, not even noticing her scars.

"My mother would love the scissors," Casita said. "But she would never have used them."

"Why not?" Mollie asked.

"Because they come from the Indaa."

Jack sat on a stool in the corner. He added in his slow English, "She liked the old ways."

"I wish I could have met her." Mollie said softly.

Casita knew that it was only because Mother was dead that they were in Mollie's kitchen. Mother would never have wanted to meet Mollie. And for that moment, Casita hated Mollie, Charles, and everyone else at Fort Clark.

Mollie took one look at Casita's face and busied herself sweeping up the hair. Finally she had a pile in the middle of the kitchen floor. "What should I do with it?"

"Fire," Jack said.

"We burn it so our grief will go into the sky," Casita said.

"That is lovely," Mollie said, brushing a tear from her cheek. She lit a piece of kindling on the stovetop with a match. They all watched until the flame flickered and finally burned strong. Taking handfuls of hair, Jack and Casita tossed it onto the stove. The hair seemed to move by itself, writhing in the flame. Then in an instant it caught in a flash of flame and was gone. The smell of burning hair filled the small kitchen, but Casita felt an easing of the tightness in her chest.

In that early morning quiet, Casita wondered if Mollie Smith was a good woman. Last night she had tried to understand how Jack and Casita needed to grieve. Would she be as open to their ways today? Or would the Indaa's ways always be more important?

No matter what, Jack and Casita must not forget who they were. When their father came, if he came, they would still be Ndé.

Jack, like any good warrior, woke instantly when he heard Mollie open the door. "I have breakfast for you in the kitchen," she said.

Outside a bugler played a lively rhythm. "That's 'Reveille,'" Mollie said brightly. Casita mouthed the word, committing it to memory. Her father had always been proud of how quick her ear was—to hear something once or twice was to remember it.

Charles was already sitting at the kitchen table, dressed in his uniform. He and Mollie discussed his day. As far as Casita could understand, Charles's work for Captain Carter was managing the assignments for every enlisted man in the cavalry.

Mollie hurried to put porridge in front of the children. As Casita tried not to gag on the sour milk, she watched

Charles carefully. He had hardly spoken to them. Casita didn't know if that was the usual way with the Indaa or if he was reconsidering letting them stay.

Jack noticed nothing, eating the food in front of him without complaint.

Finally Charles spoke to them. "Children, the prisoners are leaving this morning for the reservation at Fort Gibson in Oklahoma."

Casita saw all her plans turn to dust. What could be easier than to send Jack and her with them? She nerved herself to ask, "Do we have to go?"

"Of course not," Mollie exclaimed. "But we wondered if you wanted to see them off."

"*You* did, not *we*," Charles corrected. "I think it's a bad idea. It will only confuse the children."

To her surprise, Casita agreed with Charles. She didn't want to watch her band being exiled to Oklahoma. But she suspected Jack would see it differently.

Jack pushed his chair back with a loud squeaking sound. He stood up. "I want to go."

"What good will it do?" Casita asked in the Ndé language.

"It is our duty," he answered. "You would know that if you weren't trying so hard to make them like you."

Casita didn't want to go, but she didn't dare let Jack go alone. There was no telling what he might do out of "duty." He might jeopardize their place with Mollie and Charles. "I will come, too," she said.

An hour later, they stood with Mollie and Charles near

the guard post at the entrance to the fort. A small crowd, mainly of women, had gathered to watch the departure of the prisoners. There was no gate, a fact that had escaped her when she first entered the fort. She asked Charles why not.

"We don't need one. There are up to six hundred armed and experienced cavalry and infantry soldiers here at any time. Every Apache in Texas could attack us and they'd have no chance. Your people only win battles when they can use the terrain against us."

"Charles!" Mollie exclaimed. "That's rather tactless."

"I'm not telling her anything she doesn't know," he said with a shrug.

Six hundred men. Her father's men had never numbered more than thirty. He couldn't set them free. She was glad that Jack wasn't listening. Jack could keep his hope for a while longer.

Charles had said the prisoners would come from the stables, and Jack kept his gaze fixed in that direction. As they waited, Jack fidgeted and scratched himself where his new clothes touched his skin.

"Hold still," Casita ordered him. "You're upsetting Mollie."

"Don't tell me what to do," he answered.

"I'm just trying . . ."

"I know what you are doing. And right now I want you to leave me alone."

The morning was cool and dry. Casita heard Charles say to Mollie, "Good traveling weather."

"How far away is Fort Gibson?" Mollie asked.

"Six hundred and fifty miles, give or take," Charles said.

Casita couldn't imagine such a distance. It would take them months to travel so far.

"There!" Jack said, having spied the soldiers leading the prisoners. The children and their mothers were mounted on horseback. Even the boys that Casita knew as skilled riders slumped on the horses, staring at the ground. They had lost their pride. Someone had found them ill-fitting clothes that transformed their appearance. The Indaa clothes had such power, Casita thought, smoothing her own skirt. Only by concentrating on their faces could Casita recognize them. Most of them didn't look up. But if they did, they stared at her and Jack as though they were the enemy.

"They hate us," Jack said.

"I couldn't save everyone." Casita forced herself to keep her voice down.

"Father taught us to care for the band. We should have stayed to help them."

Casita wanted to look away, but Jack's words had stung. Her father would want her to be here. It was a small comfort, but at least these children had their mothers.

Mollie made a dismayed sound. "They're going to travel six hundred miles? They'll never make it."

Charles shifted uneasily from one foot to another. "The Army will get them there. And there will be food and shelter at the reservation."

Casita shook her head. Mollie's anger fueled hers, too. "The reservations are a slow dying for my people."

"There must be a better way," Mollie said.

Charles took her hand. "We took in these two. There's nothing else we can do."

Under his breath, so only Casita could hear, Jack said, "I wish we were going with them."

As the last of the prisoners trailed by, Casita noticed Caleb standing directly across from her. He saw her and held up an imaginary rifle and pointed it at her. With a jerk, he pretended to pull the trigger. Then he shot Jack, too. Jack's hand went to his waist, but his knife was gone. Unafraid, he started forward. Casita grabbed his shirt and held him back. She was afraid he would do something reckless.

"No, Brother," she whispered urgently. "He wants you to fight. He wants us to be sent away."

Like a good soldier, Charles noticed everything. "Ignore Caleb," he said. When Jack didn't answer, Charles put his hand on Jack's shoulder.

"Let's go home," Mollie said sadly.

"But we have no home," Jack said.

"So we make a new one," Casita said. "No matter how strange it is."

❖

Over the next few weeks, Casita thought often of her father. Once, he had told them the story of a group of Ndé who were held prisoner by the Mexicans for years. They had survived, pretending to be docile, until they could escape. The lesson, he told them, was that a Ndé could do anything to survive. Jack had replied that that was the mark of a true warrior. Father had smiled and said the bravest of the imprisoned group had been a woman. He had glanced at Mother when he said it.

At the time, Casita had wondered if Mother was the woman he meant. Had she been captured by the Mexicans? Was that why she was so insistent that captivity was worse than death? Casita tried to ask, but Mother had said she must wait until she was grown.

Now she wished she could ask Mother how to pretend to be something she wasn't, and still remain Ndé. She thought about this often, especially at night when she and Jack argued and he accused her of betraying their people. But mostly, she did whatever Mollie asked. It was safer that way.

Charles had been right when he said that the bugling set the rhythm of life at Fort Clark. "Reveille" started the day and a bugle announced almost every hour until "Taps" told them to sleep. The bugle for "Fatigue Call" was when all the soldiers were given their daily chores. It might be working in the kitchen, fetching water, repairing a roof—there was a neverending set of tasks to keep the fort running. Mollie's list of tasks was so long she joked that their "Fatigue Call" lasted all day. She did her best to keep the house clean and free of vermin, but Casita could see that the dirt and vermin were always winning. One day Mollie was in the kitchen preparing dinner while Casita sat on the front porch peeling potatoes. Mollie screamed and Casita came running.

"A snake! A huge snake!" Mollie cried.

Jack appeared from the backyard. "Where?" he asked, his eyes gleaming. He loved snakes.

"In the pot."

Carefully, Jack peered inside, Casita looking over his shoulder. A long black snake with yellow markings on its smooth scales was coiled up inside. Jack reached in and picked up a loop of the snake. It moved slowly to tighten around his wrist. "It is not poisonous," he said.

"Kill it!" Mollie screamed, backing away.

"But this snake kills rattlers," Casita said.

"I don't care!"

Scowling, Jack took the snake outside, Casita trailing after him.

"It's a good snake," he said. "I won't kill it." He stroked the head of the snake and it wrapped itself slowly about his neck. "Mollie's as bad as the soldiers. She wants anything that scares her to be dead."

"She was afraid," Casita protested. "Usually she's very kind."

As if Casita had planned it, Mollie appeared at the back door. "Jack, forget what I said. I can't kill one of God's creatures just because it terrifies me. Just take it far away."

After she had gone, Jack said, "I'm going to keep it." His expression dared Casita to argue, but she didn't bother. Jack had agreed to stay, but only on his own terms.

❖

Every day, Casita helped Mollie with the cooking, learning to use an Indaa stove. Almost all their food was either dried or out of tins. Fruits and vegetables were almost impossible to find. One morning, Casita saw firsthand how much Mollie missed fresh food. She came into the kitchen to see Mollie weeping at the table.

"What is wrong?" she asked.

Mollie emptied a bag onto the table. A dozen rotten onions spilled out. "The supply wagon came today. I paid three dollars for these onions so I could make Charles's favorite soup. But look at them!"

The word *onion* was new to Casita, but one sniff and she understood what type of plant it was. The smell took her back to that last day at El Remolino—but she shook off the memory. Thoughts of her mother only made her sad and didn't help her with her new life.

"There are wild plants that have the same taste," she said. "We could look for them. They like water. Maybe down by the springs?"

Casita had learned that the springs she had seen the day she arrived at Fort Clark supplied water to the whole fort.

Mollie didn't answer at first. She slowly washed her face

with a damp cloth. When she finally spoke, her voice was wary. "I don't think Charles would allow you to leave the fort."

Casita wasn't surprised, but it was disappointing nonetheless. With an effort, she smiled. "Maybe Charles can take both of us."

"Perhaps," Mollie answered without promising.

Casita went outside and sat on the porch. Surrounded by all these buildings of war and soldiers as far as she could see, her freedom was an illusion. No matter how kind their captors were, Jack and Casita were still prisoners. But unlike Jack, Casita was determined to be happy.

Compared to the Ndé, the Indaa lived easy. Even though she guiltily remembered how her mother hated matches, Casita loved the convenience of them. Instead of slaving over a baking stone, Casita picked up their readymade bread from the fort bakery. Even her new soft clothes smelled fresh and clean, because the cloth could be laundered. These comforts were hard to resist.

As she slowly and steadily fell into Indaa ways, Jack grew more and more bitter. Charles was the only one not pained by Jack's behavior. "That is exactly how a prisoner of war should behave," he told Mollie.

As Casita avoided Jack, Mollie grew more important to her. They became good friends. When spring gave way to early summer, they planned a garden together.

"No one can seem to grow anything here," Mollie said.

"We grew corn and squash in our village," Casita said.

"But we lived by a river and had enough water."

"I can have water brought up from the spring," Mollie said, her eyes brightening.

Casita joined in her excitement. "And if you can spare an onion, we can grow fresh ones for Charles's favorite soup."

Mollie's answering smile made Casita glad. For the first time since she had arrived at Fort Clark, she had something to look forward to.

Nde'

CHAPTER TWELVE

Aﬀter a few weeks, Mollie made an announcement. "Both of you, particularly Casita, speak English well," she said. "It's time for you to learn to read and write." Mollie was a good teacher, but she needed every drop of patience as she tried to explain the mysteries of a written language. None of the Apache bands wrote down their language. Why would they?

They were seated at a small table in the parlor and Mollie had a primer with the letters and short words for them to learn.

"So when you write down a word," Casita said slowly, "it means the same thing to everyone who reads it?"

"Yes," Mollie answered. "You can learn everything that was ever written down in a book, a letter, or a newspaper."

"We learn when we listen to our elders," Casita said. "We trust them, so we know it is true. How do we trust a writer we have never met?"

"What if he lies?" Jack asked. He didn't plan to stay long, and in the meantime he would tease Mollie.

"It is up to the reader to judge how trustworthy the writer is," Mollie said.

"But can he write anything he wants?" Casita asked.

"In this country, everyone is free to say and write what they please," Mollie said proudly.

"Even the Ndé?" Casita asked.

Mollie frowned and her voice was flat. "Not exactly. The US Government doesn't consider you citizens, so you don't have the same rights as we do."

"What does *citizen* mean?" Jack asked.

"Someone who was born here in the United States and has the right to be protected by the government."

"We were born here," Jack pointed out.

"Our people were here long before your people," Casita added.

"I know. But the government has decided you aren't citizens of America," Mollie said sadly. She pushed the primer toward them. "So learn to read and write. Show the government you can be as civilized as any citizen."

Civilized was a word that Mollie had struggled to explain. The American government claimed that civilization made them better than the Ndé. Casita was still trying to figure out why.

At first a handful of white students joined them in the parlor for afternoon lessons. They were of all ages, since the fort didn't have a school yet. But they didn't like Jack and

Casita. It didn't help that Jack would smear his face with mud like war paint and drum on the table. Even though Jack was smaller than they were, they were afraid and stopped coming to the house. Instead Mollie began teaching a class in the mess hall twice a week.

Jack hated lessons and often skipped class altogether. Sometimes Casita saw him visiting his snake in its crate underneath the cistern, but all too often he was nowhere to be found.

"Why should I learn to read?" he asked. "I should be training to fight, not to read. I want to be ready when Father comes."

Casita never told him that she had lost faith that Father would ever come. But she could use Father as a lever to force Jack to behave. "Think how pleased Father will be when you read the Indaa's words without a translator," Casita said.

"You can do it," Jack muttered. "I'm going outside."

Casita let him go and convinced Mollie it was for the best.

Despite Mollie's worry, Charles was unconcerned. "He's not trying to escape or make trouble," he said. "So let him be. I'm just glad it takes him out of the house."

Casita still worried, but there was little she could do about it. She set her mind to schoolwork. Once she could read a little, Mollie told her it was time to write the letters herself. The first time she dipped the quill into the ink and put the pen to paper, she trembled. But soon she saw that with a light touch, she could make designs on the paper. Slowly she began to draw the spider web glistening in the corner of the fireplace. The line was almost as fine and delicate as the web itself. Her hand moved faster and faster until, in her haste, she knocked over the inkwell.

Mollie saw the mess and rushed over with a cloth. "Casita! You aren't doing your letters," Mollie scolded. But she exclaimed with delight when she saw the drawing. "How lovely. For once I am glad that the spiders spin the webs faster than I can sweep them away," Mollie said with a giggle. "You have a real talent, my dear."

Satisfied that Mollie wasn't angry, Casita asked for a clean sheet of paper. From that day on, Mollie gathered every scrap of paper and colored pencil she could find. Casita drew whatever was in front of her.

Mollie gave her time in the afternoon to draw. Soon Casita was a familiar figure about the fort. Those who had previously avoided her greeted her warmly and asked to see her work. She took care to draw scenes they would like: the American flag unfurled; Captain Carter on his horse, inspecting the troops; even the privates washing dishes behind the mess hall. With her permission, Charles gave her drawings as gifts to his friends. He began to see her not as a servant or companion to Mollie, but as someone he bragged about. She was proud that he liked her work, even though she knew it was disloyal. Her parents had never encouraged her to draw.

She thought of her parents a little less as time went on. But at night sometimes, she closed her eyes and remembered home. Then when she woke, she would draw from those

116

memories. Her father. The river at El Remolino. Her favorite rock. She never drew her mother, for fear of waking her spirit again. She was happy to sketch her cousins Juanita and Miguel, because she wanted to believe they were still alive. These drawings she kept hidden from everyone, even Jack. Sometimes, when Jack accused her of becoming too "civilized," she would take out the stack of drawings. They convinced her that she was still Ndé.

Nde'

CHAPTER THIRTEEN

C ASITA HAD GROWN UP WITH HOT SUMMERS, BUT THIS ONE FELT unbearable. Maybe it was the house, which held the warmth like an oven, but Casita slept poorly, dreaming that she was an agave heart roasting under a pile of leaves and dirt. The Ndé changed their habits in the summer: they woke up earlier and napped in the afternoon. The Fort Clark bugles set the same rhythm to the day regardless of the weather and the time of year. Never had she missed the cool river mist from El Remolino more.

It was Mollie's first summer in Texas and she suffered most. She lay in the parlor, near the open window, dabbing her temple with a wet cloth. Charles and Jack pretended that the heat didn't bother them, but Casita was the one who had to wash their sweat-soaked shirts.

Casita tried to find reasons to be outside, but even in the great parade grounds she couldn't find a breeze. Enclosed on all sides by military buildings, there was no way for the wind to find the giant square. And the Army had carefully cut down every tree, so there was no shade. Even the soldiers' maneuvers—usually so precise—were listless. At night, the temperature dropped and Casita finally felt as though she could breathe. But the children's room was like a closed box, the tiny window too small to let in any cool air. One night at dinner, Jack asked if he could sleep outside.

Mollie was horrified. "There are snakes. You'll be stung by scorpions," she said. But to Casita's surprise, Charles was more sympathetic. "Jack and Casita are used to being out in the desert," he told Mollie. "Before I was injured, I loved bivouacking in the desert. Someday I must take you there, Mollie. The stars are enormous and so close you feel as though you could reach out and steal one away."

Mollie stared at him. "I had no idea you missed it so much."

"I was younger then," he said with a sigh. He glanced down at his bad leg. "But I'm sorry I didn't remember earlier. Casita and Jack grew up in the wilderness, yet we expect them to stay in that little room. It must feel like a cage."

Casita and Jack exchanged glances. The last thing either of them had expected was that Charles would understand and sympathize.

Charles went on. "Why don't I build a little porch out back? They could sleep on top of it and be perfectly safe."

Jack helped Charles build the platform. At first they worked in near silence, but eventually the shared task

119

improved their relationship. There was an ease between them.

To reach the platform, Jack and Casita climbed a ladder. When they pulled the ladder up after them, they were, as Charles promised, perfectly safe. It was much cooler. And Casita loved watching the heavens dance at night. One night Charles joined them and they taught him the Ndé names for the stars, just as their father had taught them. When Casita finally closed her eyes, she slept better than she had since she had come to Fort Clark.

One morning the sun was ahead of the bugler. Casita was wide awake watching the sun rise. Next to her, Jack was dozing, a slight snore coming from his mouth.

"Casita is doing very well, I think," Mollie said. Their sleeping space was not far from Mollie and Charles's bedroom window, open to the breeze. Casita threw back her sheet to crawl closer so she could hear better.

"She's learning to cook our kind of food. And her reading and writing are progressing."

"But not Jack's?" Charles asked with a laugh.

"He speaks English well enough, but he refuses to come to school. After he finishes his chores he just disappears. He takes an enormous lunch with him and doesn't return until dinner. I used to see him playing with that awful snake, but lately I don't know where he goes."

Casita glanced at her sleeping brother. She worried about Jack, too. Where did he go?

"Casita must know," Charles said.

"I've asked her, but she says not."

"Do you believe her?"

"Of course," Mollie said, "She's the only person I have to talk to; we've become very close." There was a long pause. "Do you think she might call me 'Mother' someday?"

Casita stiffened. She and Mollie had become friends these past weeks and she liked her more than she had thought she could ever like an Indaa. But Casita could never betray her mother's memory.

"Mollie, you mustn't forget they are still prisoners of war," Charles said slowly. "She's not your daughter."

"Until we are blessed with children of our own, I thought Casita and Jack could be our family."

Casita heard the yearning in Mollie's voice. What would happen if Mollie had a baby of her own? Would she discard Casita and Jack? And in the meantime, if Casita wouldn't be her daughter, would Mollie send them away and find another Indian to mother?

"She's practically white now," Mollie went on.

"But she's not white," Charles insisted. "She never will be. And Jack certainly will always be Apache. Your experiment has been successful, but don't expect too much. Not even you can completely take the Indian out of those kids."

"I'm not finished yet," Mollie said with confidence. "You know what I believe. The solution to the Indian problem is—"

"—love." Charles said the last word with her and they both laughed.

Casita heard them getting out of bed and she quickly

121

crawled back to her blanket. She glanced at Jack and saw he was awake.

"So your Mollie thinks we are the Indian problem," he said bitterly. "She doesn't care about us; we are an experiment."

"No," Casita said quickly. "You heard her. She thinks of us as her own children."

"Until she has her own," he shot back. "What then? Your plan kept us alive, but what kind of life is it? We pretend to be like them. And they pretend we are not Ndé." He sat up and pulled on his shirt.

"You try so hard to be one of them that you forget you are not," he said. "But Charles hasn't forgotten. To him we are savages."

"Where are you going?" she asked, as he tugged his boots onto his feet.

"I'm going someplace where I can be Ndé." He swung his body down the ladder and disappeared in the greyish morning.

"Jack!" Casita didn't dare raise her voice in case Mollie and Charles heard. What did he mean? Where could he be Ndé? Surely nowhere in the fort. She had a bad feeling that he was doing something stupid. Or dangerous. Or both. She had to stop him. She pulled on her moccasins and hurried down the ladder. She reached the ground just in time to see Jack slip behind the water tanks behind the house. He carried a knapsack that he hadn't had before. *Please don't try to run away*, she thought.

Moving as silently as he was, she followed him. He darted

from one outbuilding to another, circling the edge of the fort until he reached the place where the ground fell away to the spring below. She saw his silhouette, barely more than a shadow against the sky, and then he abruptly disappeared.

"Jack!" she cried. Had he fallen? She hurried over. The hill was steep, but it wasn't a sheer drop. If you knew how to look, there was a trail, barely noticeable, in the brush. She looked round. The area was deserted—these outbuildings were rarely used. She was at the edge of the fort's land. When Jack went down the hill, he had left Fort Clark. As Charles would say, he was absent without leave. Was this where he went every day? Why? What could be so important to him that he would risk Charles's anger?

She had to know. After making sure there was no one to see her, she plunged down the hill.

Halfway, she slowed when she saw a small group of huts with mud roofs along the creek. Several dark-skinned Indians of all ages were moving about. This must be where the Seminole scouts lived with their families. She saw a tall, familiar figure. It was Seminole Jim. She hadn't seen him since that night on the trail from El Remolino. In fact, she hardly ever saw the scouts. They kept to themselves and didn't train with the rest of the soldiers. They weren't welcome in the mess hall either.

The boys welcomed Jack like he was an old friend. He opened his knapsack and handed rolls from the bakery to the youngest children. Was that why he was here? To feed the children? Charles and Mollie would never allow that.

Jack would never admit it, but she was almost as skilled as him at remaining unseen, so she tucked herself away in the brush so she could watch. It was the only way to find out what mattered so much to her little brother. Spying on him from up here reminded her of her favorite rock. But the circumstances were different.

Jack and some of the boys quickly paired off and began wrestling. *Ah, he's training*, Casita thought. Of course. Casita had watched such scenes more times than she could remember; it was how the Ndé boys were taught to fight. She had rooted for Jack to win ever since he started.

The two boys grappled each other, each seeking to trip the other or use his weight against him and bring him to the ground. When Jack was slammed on his side, Casita flinched for him. When Jack turned the tables and pinned his opponent, she had to stifle a cheer. Even among the Seminoles, Jack was still very good. He bested several boys before finally falling before a boy who towered over him. Father had taught him well.

When the wrestling was done, Seminole Jim handed out knives to each of the boys. When Jack took one, Casita buried her head in her hands. "Jack, you are a fool," she breathed. She shuddered to think what Charles would say if he caught Jack with a knife.

The boys threw their knives at a target. Over and over again. The thump of the knives slamming into the wood brought her back to the clearing at El Remolino where the children trained. She had practiced her bow and arrow there, and knife skills, too. Every Ndé child could defend herself. Even though she was angry with Jack for jeopardizing everything she had worked for, she understood why he had. He must have missed this training most of all.

Once Seminole Jim was satisfied with their progress, he took the knives back.

Casita decided she had seen enough and she climbed up the hill. The sun was rising in the sky and the climb was difficult. She was trying to catch her breath when she reached the top of the ridge and forgot to be cautious.

The sun was in her eyes. She blinked and then somehow the sun went away and she was in shadow. A tall figure loomed over her. "Wait until I tell Lieutenant Smith that you tried to escape." Caleb grinned at the prospect. "You'll be at Fort Gibson before the week is out."

"I did not try to escape," Casita insisted. "I'm still here."

"I knew you couldn't be trusted," he said. "You bided your time until you thought no one was looking. But I kept my eye on you."

What did he suspect? Had he seen Jack, too?

He advanced on her, not taking his eyes from her face. "The Smiths think they're being so good by taking you in. . . . They're just letting a pair of coyotes into the henhouse. Are you trying to get a message to your tribe? Are you telling them about our defenses?"

She stepped back. Her heels were on the edge of the steep

drop. A quick shove from Caleb and she'd be lucky not to be seriously hurt. He thought she was a danger; he'd do it just to protect the fort. "Our tribe is gone. Your army killed them. Let me alone."

"Not until you tell me what were you doing out here," he said suspiciously.

Edging forward to firmer ground, Casita thought quickly. "Drawing." She pulled out the little notebook she always kept in her skirt pocket.

"Let me see that." He grabbed it from her and flipped through the pages. He ignored all the portraits she'd done and found sketches of the fort. "You're spying on us. You're giving this information to the Apaches."

"It's a picture of the mess hall," she said. "Not dangerous at all." She took another step forward and tried to put him on the defensive. "What are you doing here? Shouldn't you be on duty?"

He craned his neck to look past her and see where she had been. "What's down there?" he asked, not budging.

"A pretty view." Casita had to divert his attention away from Jack and the Seminoles. "Excuse me, but I have to go back to Mrs. Smith. You could take me there and talk to her about my dangerous pictures." Anything to get him away from here.

"I won't be seen with a dirty Indian," he said. He was sure he had caught her doing something wrong, but he wasn't sure what.

"Do as you like," she said, finally moving beyond him.

This time he let her go, but when she looked back, he was still watching her. Her quick walk was almost a run, and she didn't stop until she reached the parade grounds.

A regiment was drilling with bayonets. The soldiers ran toward stuffed dummies and stabbed them with the blades attached to their rifles. The thudding noise reminded her of Jack's knives. Captain Carter was commanding the drill. "Again!" he shouted. Her stomach clenched. What was she doing here, living among soldiers who practiced to fight Indians like her? Caleb might be the only one to say so, but they all hated her kind. In Mollie's house it was easy to forget that she and Jack were surrounded by enemies. Which was exactly why Jack had to avoid attracting their attention. She'd tell him so as soon as he came home.

Jack didn't return until dinner. After the meal, Mollie and Charles sat on the front porch watching the Retreat Parade. Casita held her tongue until she and Jack were doing the dishes.

"You are a fool," she accused, shoving the dishes into soapy water.

He handed her the tin cups. "Why?"

"I saw you today at the Seminole camp. You are training there."

"How dare you follow me?" Jack demanded.

"It is a good thing I did," she said, scrubbing the dishes hard. "I don't want to be sent to the reservation for what you did. You must not go there again."

"If I can't be with the Ndé, the scouts are the closest I can find," Jack said. "I must train so Father won't be disappointed when he comes."

Of course, she thought. *He's doing this for Father.* She turned to him, drying her hands on a towel. She had to be honest with him. "Father isn't coming," she said. "It's been too long. And even if he did, he couldn't rescue us."

"Father can do anything." Jack said.

She grabbed his arm and took him outside and around the corner where they could see the parade ground. The band was playing and the troops were marching back and forth across the parade ground at double time. The rifles were polished and the brass insignia on their uniforms shone in the setting sun. "Look at them. All the Ndé and all their allies aren't enough to fight them. We are a handful of sand against a whole desert."

The soldiers had finished the march and been dismissed by Captain Carter before Jack spoke. "Better to die with honor than to give up," he said.

"I haven't given up," Casita said slowly.

"You've done worse. You're becoming one of them. Before the raid, you would have been proud of me for finding a way to continue to train. Now when you talk, you sound like Charles and Mollie. Where is my sister?"

"I'm right here," she said. The soldiers had quickly disappeared and the Parade Ground was almost empty. But they would return to train the next morning. They drilled every day without fail. They wouldn't stop until the Ndé were dead. Jack dreamed of honor, while Casita only hoped to keep them alive. How could she make him listen? "It's too dangerous."

"I've been there every day for weeks," Jack said. "It's safe."

She hesitated, knowing he would be angry once she confessed. "Not anymore," she said. "Caleb followed me today."

"You led him to me—how could you be so careless?"

"I'm sorry. But watch out for him. He'll make trouble for you, Brother."

"If he does, he will be sorry," Jack retorted.

"He's older and heavier than you," she warned.

"But I am a Ndé warrior."

That is exactly what you must not be, she thought sadly. But no matter how she tried to change him, Jack would always be a warrior of the Ndé. It was Casita who had forgotten who she was.

Nde'

CHAPTER FOURTEEN

THE NEXT MORNING, CASITA LEFT THE HOUSE TO FETCH THE BREAD from the fort bakery. She timed the chore for when most of the soldiers were in the mess hall. She preferred not to see them drilling with their bayonets or rifles. Walking around the perimeter of the enormous parade square, she realized that she now looked only at the path in front of her and felt small. When had she forgotten to look around her and off into the distance?

Lost in her thoughts, she jumped when she heard Caleb's voice in her ear. "I know what your brother was doing yesterday," he said before he shoved past her.

Casita watched him walk away. If Caleb really knew about Jack, he wouldn't keep quiet. She was sure of that. She hurried home to warn Jack, but of course he wasn't there. All day long she waited for the axe to fall. Mollie had to scold her several times for not paying attention to her lessons.

Evening came and Casita began to hope that the danger would not come.

Rat-a-tat.

Sitting with her embroidery in the parlor, Casita stared at the door, willing whoever was there to go away.

Rat-a-tat.

"Casita, why don't you answer the door?" Mollie called from the kitchen.

Reluctantly, Casita forced herself to open the front door. Captain Carter was standing there, filling the doorway with bad news. "Good evening. I'd like to see Lieutenant Smith and his wife, please."

A few minutes later, Casita pressed her ear against the door to the parlor, but she could only make out the muffled voices of Charles and Captain Carter. She raced out the back door to circle round to the front of the house where the parlor windows were open. She crawled onto the porch and crouched under the window to listen.

"What are you doing?" Jack asked.

"Where have you been?" she whispered. "Never mind. Listen!"

"Is it about me?" he asked. After she nodded, he joined her under the window.

Captain Carter was in mid-sentence: "—reported that the boy—"

"Jack," Mollie supplied.

"—Jack has been seen in the Seminole camp. Outside the fort."

Next to her, she felt Jack's body go still.

"Only *just* outside," Mollie argued. "And he wasn't trying to escape."

"No, no," Captain Carter said hurriedly. "There's no question of that. But he was practicing with knives and those axes they carry."

"Surely that is just boys playing games," Mollie said.

Charles contradicted her. "Mollie, this is serious."

"You see, Mrs. Smith," Captain Carter said, "knife contests and the like are how the Indians train their boys to fight our men. Why else would he learn knife skills? You can see why I'm concerned."

"I will speak to him immediately," Charles said.

"And confine him to quarters unless he is with you or your wife," the captain insisted.

Jack started to speak, but Casita placed her hand on his arm to quiet him. There was movement inside as if the captain were getting to his feet. Casita and Jack scurried back into the kitchen.

"You see what you've done!" Jack accused. "I've lost the only thing that made living here bearable."

Casita was relieved and told him so. "You could have been sent away."

"What difference does it make now?" he muttered. They both looked up guiltily when Charles appeared at the kitchen door.

"Jack, come into the parlor. I have to talk to you." Jack

followed Charles. Mollie stood in the doorway, pulling back so Jack could pass. As Casita watched him disappear, she hardly noticed that Mollie had come to sit with her.

"Did you know Jack was playing with the Seminole children?" Mollie asked.

There was no point in lying; Mollie already knew. "I only found out yesterday. I told him not to go again."

Putting her arm around Casita's shoulders, Mollie squeezed. "You are a good girl, my dear."

Casita had to think about that word, "good." A good Ndé girl would be proud of her brother's resourcefulness, not ashamed. A good Indaa girl, on the other hand, might betray her brother's confidence to keep peace in the house. Did Casita know which kind of good girl she really was?

For the next few days, Jack refused to speak with anyone and even moved back into their hot stuffy room. Casita's relief soon turned to irritation. Mollie was frustrated, too. One sweltering evening they were sitting on the front porch to watch the sunset. Silhouetted against the sun, a defiant Jack stood in the corner of the tiny yard, kicking the dirt.

"Can't you do something?" Mollie asked Charles.

"What do you expect me to do?" he asked reasonably. "He broke the rules and he's being punished. I'd be more concerned if he were happy."

"That is not helpful."

"I remember once I refused to speak to my mother for a week. I can't even remember why." Charles chuckled.

"I have some sympathy for your mother," Mollie replied. "It's too hot to have him always brooding in the corners. Can you find something for him to do outside the house?"

"He likes horses," Casita said. Usually she let them talk and she just listened, but this was a chance to make amends to Jack.

Charles considered. "I could find him some work in the stables."

"That would be wonderful," Casita said.

"But we don't want to reward him for misbehaving," Mollie said worriedly.

"Make up your mind, Mollie. Do you want him out of the house or suitably punished? Besides, I think he's suffered enough."

Casita and Mollie exchanged surprised glances. Usually Charles was a stickler for the rules.

"Think how dull life must be for the boy. I'm not surprised he went looking for friends," Charles said. "I'll talk to the stable master."

Charles took Jack to the stable the next afternoon, and he began working the following day. At dinner every night, he was more talkative than Charles and Mollie had ever seen, raving about the quality of the horses and telling stories about their little quirks.

"The 4th Cavalry has some of the finest horseflesh in the Army," Charles agreed.

Once Jack was busy and happy, the house began to feel more like a home. And the Smiths and Jack and Casita felt a little more like a family. Jack began to make friends with the stable boys, although the soldiers were still wary of the Apache boy. When Jack complained to Casita that they ignored him, she was stunned. Didn't he remember what those same soldiers had done to them?"

"We were at war then," he said pityingly. "But I'm here now, and I could learn a lot if they would only talk to me."

So Jack wanted to continue training as a fighter, but with the only fighters available to him: the 4th Cavalry riders. It made sense, she supposed, but something felt wrong. It was one thing to accept Mollie's help, another to befriend the soldiers who had massacred your village.

"The soldiers will never accept you, so it does not matter," she answered practically.

"They might if I give them a good reason."

"What do you mean?" she asked.

"Wait and see, Sister," he said with a mischievous grin.

That grin made her worry most. He was too reckless. What might he do to try to be noticed by the soldiers? She watched him closely for the next few days—even spying on him at the stable—until he told her to stop.

One morning when she was washing up after breakfast, Jack handed her the last plate and asked very casually, "Will you and Mollie be sewing on the porch this afternoon?"

Casita gave him a hard look, but he returned it with an

innocent expression that made her more suspicious. "We will. Why?"

Smiling, he said, "There's no reason." And then he left for the stables.

Casita thought all day about what he might do. And that afternoon she made sure that she and Mollie did their needlepoint on the front porch where they had an excellent view of the parade ground. Mollie was patient as she tried to teach Casita how to sew, but Casita struggled with the fine thread and the tiny needle. Today, Casita was distracted. What did Jack have planned?

Finally Casita saw Jack lead an enormous horse to one corner of the square where new horses were often trained. Casita pointed him out to Mollie and they both put aside their sewing.

Jack looked tiny next to the skittish horse. Cavalry horses were trained to be calm, but this gelding shied at every unfamiliar noise. Jack handled him well until he handed the reins to Corporal Brody, who trained the new horses. Brody adjusted the stirrup irons and hoisted himself into the saddle. With a shrill whinny like a human scream, the horse sank back on his rear legs.

"Whoa, boy!" Brody shouted.

The horse bucked forward, kicking first his front legs out and then his back. Brody was thrown off. The riderless horse took off at a gallop, barreling through a group of soldiers who flung themselves out of the way. Not Jack, though. He sprinted after the animal.

"Look!" Mollie cried. "It's our Jack."

Watching with suspicious eyes, Casita said, "I see." This must be something he had planned, but she didn't see how.

Jack was a fast runner. He came alongside the beast and grabbed its mane to swing atop the animal. Oddly, Jack didn't lower himself into the saddle. Instead he shifted his weight to the horse's shoulders and calmly rode back to Brody. The soldiers cheered and applauded. When Jack dismounted, Brody pounded Jack's back in approval. "Well done, son!"

Mollie clapped as loud as the rest. "That was so brave!"

"Yes, it certainly was," Casita said slowly.

That evening, she confronted Jack. "Brother, how did that horse just happen to go wild at that moment?"

"There might have been a metal spur under the saddle," he admitted slyly.

"So when Brody mounted . . ." Casita worked it out. "But then how did you ride it back?"

"Maybe I was careful not to put any weight on the saddle."

Jack had been clever. Father would have approved heartily. It was the kind of stratagem he would have liked. "But why did you do it?" she asked.

"The soldiers like me now," he said simply. "I told you I could do it."

After that, Jack only worked with the most difficult horses, and he became a favorite with the best riders. One night at dinner Charles called him their mascot. Casita wasn't sure what that meant, but Charles seemed pleased. So did Jack.

"Are you sure this is wise?" Mollie said. "They are so much older than he is."

"The Army is like that. We are a band of brothers," Charles explained. "Jack has replaced his old family with a new one."

Nde'

CHAPTER FIFTEEN

THE HOUSEHOLD WAS CONTENT NOW THAT JACK WAS SATISFIED with his new life. Everything was going so well that Casita let down her guard, but she should have known that Jack could not stay docile for long.

Sunday was the day that most of the soldiers were off duty, either resting or drinking in town or playing games. One hot Sunday afternoon, Casita followed Jack to the end of the parade ground. A group of soldiers were unloading a crate and setting up for a game of baseball. Casita knew that teams were made up of nine people, but this day there were dozens of people milling about. Seminole Jim was there, too, with a young boy who must have been his son.

One of the team captains greeted Jack. "Jacko! I'm glad you could come. We need someone with your speed."

Jacko? When had Jack lost his name?

Jack nodded happily before running to the crate to pull

out the bases, tossing them to the other players. Casita was reminded how the boys at El Remolino had fetched axes and knives for the warriors, desperately trying to attract their attention and favor. Jack was doing well.

"Casita, bring the bats to home base," he said. Casita had never had a chance to see the bats up close. As she laid them out in a row by the base, she ran her hands over the smooth wood of the whittled branches.

"This is an American game," a low voice said behind her. "For whites only."

She knew it was Caleb. She had heard from Mollie that he had accompanied a patient to an Army hospital back East, and she had hoped he would stay there.

"I don't understand why you and your brother are still here. You're like cats with nine lives. You should be dead or on the reservation by now."

There was nothing she could say to make him hate her less, so she turned away. He grabbed her arm. Instantly, Jack was at her side. "Leave my sister alone," he said. He only came up to Caleb's shoulder, but Caleb dropped Casita's arm—but not before he added, "No Indians allowed."

Passing by, the team captain said, "You've got that wrong. I want Jack on my team."

The captain was an officer—baseball was one of the few pastimes that officers and enlisted men shared—so Caleb didn't dare speak his mind. Waiting until the captain had moved away, Caleb stepped close to Jack and pulled back his arm to punch him.

Jack had plenty of time to dodge the blow, but he let the punch land on his mouth. Suddenly all the players were watching. A fight was as good a distraction as a baseball game.

Jack's lip was bleeding but he was smiling. Casita knew he couldn't have planned this, but somehow she knew this was exactly what he wanted.

Jack called to Casita in English, "Sister, some water."

Seminole Jim gave her his canteen. As she passed it to Jack, she asked, "Are you sure about this?"

"I know what I am doing." Jack faced the crowd and took a long swallow of the water, almost as though it were part of a ceremony.

Caleb put up his fists, but Jack was too quick. Jack closed in early and landed a sharp blow to the bridge of Caleb's nose. Blood covered Caleb's mouth and chin. He staggered, wiping the blood away with the back of his hand.

"Yes!" Casita shouted. Caleb had frightened her for too long.

Jack's fists slammed against Caleb's rib cage until Caleb fell to the ground. In an instant, Jack was on his chest, one hand round his throat. He held up the other arm above his head. The onlookers cheered and Seminole Jim declared Jack the winner.

Jack leapt to his feet. Making sure he had everyone's attention, he spat out the water he had taken before the fight. It was a Ndé training technique to complete some feat—a sparring match, a run up a steep hill—and not swallow the water. Casita grinned. Good for Jack! The soldiers took a moment longer to understand; then they roared with approval. They put Jack on their shoulders and paraded around the baseball field. Jack was a hero.

Caleb remained on the ground, humiliated.

Casita did not like Caleb. He had tormented her, but now she felt sorry for him. He had no idea how skilled a Ndé warrior was, even one as young as Jack. She went over to Caleb and offered him her hand.

"Stay away from me!" he said, batting her hand away. "I don't need help from a filthy Indian." He clambered to his feet and his nose started gushing blood.

"You once helped me when I was hurt," she said.

"I should have let you die."

"But you didn't. You brought me to Mollie Smith."

"I can't believe she's still fooled by you. Letting you live in her house, feeding you like you're her kin. . . . Doesn't she know who you really are?"

Casita dropped her hand and started to walk away.

"Your own mother didn't even want you . . ."

Casita stopped, and slowly turned around. "You know nothing about me!"

He jabbed at her shoulder and neck. "I know more than you think. I know who tried to kill you at Remolino."

"It was a soldier," Casita insisted. "During the battle!"

"I wonder if you believe that or if you just can't help lying? I know it was your mother."

Casita shook her head. A remembered pain was stabbing at her scalp and shoulders. "No it wasn't. She was dead."

"I talked to the sergeant who killed your mother."

Casita remembered that soldier only too well. She remembered the look in his eyes as he aimed his pistol at Mother's body. She put her head in her hands, trying to make the pain stop.

Caleb went on, "He said your own mother brought a rock down on your head and neck. Not once but three times!"

Casita's fingers were rubbing her scars. Three of them. What exactly did she remember? Her mother had been shot. Casita had been crawling on her knees, away from the battle, trying desperately to reach the safety of the hills. In that moment, when her back was turned, she felt a sharp pain at the top of her back. In her head. Then she remembered nothing at all.

"You're worthless," Caleb said viciously. "Even your own mother hated you."

Slowly and deliberately, she said, "I am glad my brother beat you and shamed you in front of everyone."

Caleb's bluster seemed to disappear like rain in the desert.

Casita walked away, toward home. She felt dizzy, as though she had fallen from a great height and hit the ground hard.

Caleb's words made her question everything she knew. She remembered her mother so clearly: tall and serene, roasting agave hearts. Her strong fingers braiding Casita's hair. Her calm voice reassuring Casita about the Changing Woman ceremony. How could that mother hurt her? But Mother hated the Indaa. She had died rather than be taken

143

prisoner. Had she wanted Casita to die too? How dare she try to take Casita's life? She wanted to strike out at her mother, but she was long dead. Casita's loyalty to her had been the thing that still lived.

The Smiths' house was in front of her now. Mollie was sitting on the porch, shucking some of the early peas Casita had coaxed out of the ground. Mollie waved. "Look at what's happening!" She put the peas aside and pointed to the soldiers' barracks. The soldiers found an old blanket and four of them each took a corner and spread it out tight. Then another soldier tossed Jack onto the blanket.

"It's a sign they have accepted him," Mollie said. "They do it for all the new recruits. Jack is truly one of them now."

One of them. Jack had done exactly what she had insisted he do—he had adapted to life among the Indaa. He wore their clothes and spoke their language. And he had managed to become a warrior by combining his traditions with theirs.

"I never thought he would do this well," Mollie said. "Charles will be so happy. Isn't it wonderful?"

Casita had been so loyal to her mother that she had never properly appreciated this kind woman.

She grabbed Mollie's hand and said, "Yes, it is . . . Mama."

PART THREE

Nde'

"In Indian civilization I am a Baptist, because I believe in immersing the Indian in our civilization and when we get them under, holding them there until they are thoroughly soaked."

—*Richard H. Pratt*
Founder of the
Carlisle Indian Industrial School

Nde'

CHAPTER SIXTEEN

February 1880 (three years later)

THE BUGLE SOUNDED "REVEILLE" BEFORE CASITA FINISHED TYING her second shoe.

"Jack, I think you cheated," she muttered to herself. For the last six months, Jack had played the tune to wake up the camp. Charles, who had once played with the Regimental Band, had taught him the instrument. Casita had always disliked how the Army acted as if the sun wouldn't rise without the lively tune, but once Jack was bugling, it had become a private game between them. Could Casita wake and dress on her own before Jack put the bugle to his lips? He had won this time.

She looked around her room to check that everything was spick and span—an expression Charles had taught her. Keeping it clean was much easier now that Mollie had insisted Casita have a room to herself. Jack had made himself a shelter on the platform and stayed there year-round. Casita's bed was neatly made and her clothes folded and put away. Charles would inspect it later; he liked to say she was in the US Army now. Casita decorated her room with her own drawings: horses on parade, Mollie's flowers in the yard, even Jack's trumpet. On the small table next to her bed was a picture she had just started. It was to be a surprise for Mollie.

Casita hurried to the kitchen to start the stove. Mollie was expecting a baby and Casita liked to make her hot tea every morning. She also prepared the porridge on the stove and brought in the milk from the icebox on the porch.

"You are a godsend," Mollie said, accepting the hot beverage gratefully. She maneuvered herself onto a chair. The baby had already grown big, even though the birth was not for another month. Casita hadn't believed her when Mollie had pointed to a date on the calendar and said that was the day the baby would come. Only the Indaa would try to put a timetable on a baby as if it were the stagecoach. Among the Ndé, the baby came when it wanted to. A mother would only start preparing a cradleboard in the last days before it arrived. But Charles had already built a crib, and Mollie had knitted half a dozen blankets.

At first Casita had worried that the date on the calendar was also the day that Mollie would send them away. After all, she and Jack had been temporary substitutes for Mollie's own children. When she had finally found the courage to ask, Mollie had been shocked. Angry, even. "Casita, my baby is the luckiest in the world. He—or she—already has a wonderful big sister and brother."

As Casita set the table, Mollie watched her over the steaming mug. "Look at your hair," she said. "It's grown so long. How long has it been since you cut it?"

"Almost three years." Her braided hair went to the middle of her back now. Casita didn't like to remember why she had cut it. She had become quite good at forgetting her mother. "I missed it when it was short."

"Jack has kept his hair short like the soldiers," Mollie said. "Charles says in a few years, Jack could enlist. I wish he would think of doing something else. One military man is enough for this family."

"He's still very young," Casita said. Mollie guessed that Jack was eleven or twelve now. Among the Ndé, the number of summers mattered less than what you accomplished. A Ndé boy was considered an adult and a warrior after he participated in four raids. Maybe that was why Jack wanted to be a soldier.

A Ndé girl grew up after her Changing Woman ceremony. Casita's monthly bleeding had come the previous year. Mollie had been very matter-of-fact, teaching Casita how to clean her underthings and how to make herself more comfortable. She had also insisted Casita sleep in her own room.

For the Indaa, the passage to being a woman was only a physical change. There was nothing spiritual about it. Casita would never dance in the Changing Woman ceremony. She was a woman now, but without the ceremony, she was forever apart from the Ndé. An exile. Casita had been afraid of the ceremony when she was younger, but now she regretted that she had missed it.

She wondered if any of the girls in her family were still alive to do the ritual. Had Juanita survived the raid? She knew the Army still hunted the Lipan Apaches, but they found fewer and fewer of them these days. Charles thought that meant they were dead, but Seminole Jim had told her that the survivors were hidden in Mexico. If that were true, how would Juanita have her ceremony?

Casita shook her head to rid herself of these sad thoughts. She had made her choice. Her history might be Ndé, but her future lay with the Indaa. She was a white girl with dark skin. Whenever she found herself mourning the past, she pressed on the scars at her neck and scalp until they hurt. They were the perfect reminder that her old life was filled with pain.

"Is there coffee for me, Casita?" Charles asked her from the doorway.

"Here, Papa," she said, pouring him a cup from the metal coffee pot. She wrinkled her nose; no matter how long she had lived with the Smiths, she had never developed a taste for it.

"I need some, too," Jack said, coming in from outside. He had grown at least half a foot in the last three years, and he was the same height as Casita now. He put his trumpet case on the table and rubbed his cold hands together. "My lips almost froze on the trumpet."

"This isn't cold at all!" Mollie said. "In Pennsylvania, where I grew up, it gets so cold that the windows are covered with ice."

Casita and Jack grinned. To them, Mollie's stories of faraway Pennsylvania sounded like fairy tales.

"If we ever visit," Charles said, "we'll be sure to go in winter. I'd like you to see snow. And I bet Jack would be a natural at ice skating."

Jack looked questioningly at Casita. She lifted her shoulders; she didn't know what ice skating was either.

As Casita handed Jack his coffee, she whispered, "Are you sure the sun had risen before you played 'Reveille,' Brother?"

"The sun looked like it was up to me," he said. "You just have to be quicker."

Jack left soon to go to the stables. After she finished her chores, schoolwork was always the highlight of Casita's day. Casita and Mollie were hard at work on geography that afternoon. Mollie had borrowed a map of the United States and was showing Casita how the country had expanded westward.

"It's out of date," Mollie apologized. "It's from before the war. Nevada and Nebraska are still territories here, not states."

"And we are here?" Casita put her palm over the large wedge shape that was labeled *Texas*.

Mollie nodded. "And I come from there." She pointed to a long rectangle in the upper right-hand side that was labeled *Pennsylvania*.

151

Casita barely glanced at Pennsylvania; it was the map of Texas that fascinated her. She traced her finger on the squiggly line between Texas and Mexico. "The Great River," she said.

"The Rio Grande," Mollie corrected.

The land south of the river was blank, as though the mapmaker only cared about the United States.

"What about Mexico?" Casita asked.

Mollie looked surprised. "I can ask if there is a Mexican map we can borrow. Would you would like to see where you came from?"

"No, it's not important," Casita said shortly. She did not want to see El Remolino, even if it were only a tiny printed name on a map. To look back was to risk being hurt again. So Casita changed the subject: "This blue on either side—that is water?" It must be an illusion of the mapmaker; there was no possible way the world could hold so much water and not drown.

Mollie smiled and nodded. "I've never seen the Pacific, but I saw the Atlantic Ocean once."

Casita put the tip of her finger on tiny Maine, up in the northeast corner. Then she walked her fingers across the whole great land until she reached Texas. Texas had been Apache land. And the Comanches had come from the north in Oklahoma. Here was New Mexico, where the Mescaleros lived. Her finger trotted up to the Dakotas. This was Sioux country—Charles was always talking about how much trouble the Sioux gave the Army. Finally she made it to California with its huge ocean. She guessed that every part of this map

152

had once belonged to Indians. The Indaa had started with a little sliver of Eastern land and had taken everything in their path until they reached the opposite side.

Casita was so intent on the map, she didn't hear the knock at the door.

"Captain Carter!" Mollie exclaimed with pleasure when she opened the door. Casita was not pleased; to her, he would always represent the worst the Army could do. She didn't trust him. Casita started to excuse herself.

"No, Casita, you should stay," he said. "What I have to say concerns you, too."

Mollie and Casita sensed it was not good news. Casita and Jack were technically prisoners of war, even if they didn't think of themselves that way. The Army could exercise its power over them anytime it chose. They sat down on the sofa opposite him and prepared for the worst.

"Go ahead, Captain," Mollie said.

"Have you heard about a fellow called Lieutenant Pratt who is opening up a school at the Carlisle barracks in Pennsylvania?" he asked. "It's a school for Indian children." His eyes rested on Casita.

Casita stared back. She didn't want to go to an Indian school, now that she didn't feel Indian anymore.

"I've heard of it," Mollie said slowly. "The Quakers are interested in the lieutenant's experiment." She smiled. "Pratt has an idea that the Indians can be educated as well as any white child." She took Casita's hand. "We could have told him that."

Casita squeezed Mollie's hand tightly, holding on for her life. Mollie and Charles would never let them go, would they?

"Pratt wants to teach them a trade, too," Captain Carter said.

"I think that's a wonderful idea," Mollie exclaimed. "Casita is such a help to me, especially now that I'm in a family way."

"Mrs. Smith, I think you are deliberately not taking my meaning," the captain said. "Pratt needs students. Lots of them. We've been ordered to send as many as we can find. Casita and Jack are on the list."

"They are my children. And I won't let them go," Mollie said, suddenly fierce. "You can't let us love them for three years then take them away without any warning!"

Like a mama bear defending her cubs, Casita thought sadly. But a bear couldn't win against the Army, and neither could Mollie.

"Officially, ma'am, they aren't your children," he said sternly. "They are prisoners of war and their fate is decided by the US Army. They leave next week."

Mollie gasped. Casita cleared her throat to interrupt the way Mollie had taught her. "Captain, may I ask a question?"

"Of course."

"What if I don't want to go?" She shrank into the corner of the sofa as though it might swallow her up.

"You don't have a choice."

"I didn't have a choice at El Remolino either," Casita said, struggling not to cry.

"That was a long time ago," Captain Carter said. "And this situation is different. This school is a new idea. It may be the solution to the Indian problem, and you will be there at the beginning."

She had not heard the words "Indian problem" in a long time. Until the Indaa came to Texas, there had never been an Indian problem. The white people had created it themselves and now wanted her to suffer for it by taking her family away again. An anger that Casita had not felt since that day when the soldiers destroyed her village welled up in her.

"If I refuse to go will you tie to me to a horse again?" Casita asked angrily. "Beat my brother until he agrees? Maybe you'd like to burn down my house again? Because that was how you tried to solve the Indian problem before!"

"Casita!" Mollie cried.

Captain Carter held up a hand to reassure Mollie. "Ma'am, the girl is upset. Understandably. I know she has been happy here. And young Jack has done a fine job with the horses. But it is only for a few years, then they can come back."

Casita took no comfort in that; the Army was not to be trusted.

"Isn't there anything we can do?" Mollie asked. "Someone we can talk to?"

"I have my orders."

There was no use trying to fight it, Casita knew. No one argued with the Army. Her life here with Mollie and Charles was over. Everything she had thought she had won was like a mirage in the desert. The only thing that was real

155

was Mollie's hand holding hers. Casita pulled away. Better to make the break quickly.

"May I please be excused," Casita mumbled. Without waiting for Mollie's response, she ran out of the room. In the kitchen, she stood with her back to the stove, out of breath. The scars on her neck began to throb.

The Army had destroyed her life. Again.

Nde'

CHAPTER SEVENTEEN

"Mollie, for heaven's sake, isn't she packed yet?" Charles's bellow came from the parlor. "The stagecoach leaves in an hour."

"Almost!" Mollie called from Casita's room.

"But we are finished," Casita said. Her canvas bag was packed with all her clothes.

"Not quite," Mollie said. "Captain Carter said you could bring some keepsakes of home to Carlisle. What about this?" She pulled out Casita's first needlepoint. It wasn't very expertly done, but Mollie and Casita had worked on it together.

"Home sweet home," Casita said, swallowing hard to get rid of the lump in her throat.

Trying to be lighthearted, Mollie said, "Unless you look closely, you can't see the specks of blood from when you pricked your fingers. You can take a little bit of home with you."

Casita nodded. "But I'm coming back."

"Captain Carter said you can come home in three years. That's not really so long."

Casita had been with Mollie for three years, and it felt like a lifetime.

"It will be good for you," Mollie continued. "You'll find new teachers for your art. And won't it be nice to meet other Indian children? You could find a friend your own age."

"Mollie!"

"Coming, Charles!" Mollie hesitated, then reached into her pocket. "There is one more thing I want you to have."

Casita caught her breath when Mollie gave her the leather necklace and the shell hanging from it. "My necklace," she whispered. "I thought it was gone."

"Captain Carter wanted us to destroy anything that was Apache," Mollie said hesitantly. "But I put it away for you. I wasn't sure if you would want it."

It was too painful to hold it; the memories of her father would overwhelm her. "I don't want it anymore," Casita said, handing it back. "It's from a time of my life that I chose to give up." Not that her choices had mattered much in the end, she thought.

"I never meant for you to feel like you had to forget your past," Mollie said. "There will be so many different tribes at Carlisle, you should have something that represents your own people. Something to remember them by."

"I don't want to remember," she said fiercely.

"Memories of good things cannot hurt you," Mollie said, pressing the necklace into Casita's palm. "And one day it might bring you comfort."

"I don't want to leave you," Casita said.

Mollie put her arms around Casita. "You will come back to us," she whispered.

But Casita couldn't help thinking that Mollie was making a promise she couldn't keep.

❖

Exactly an hour later, they stood by the stagecoach at the entrance to the fort.

"Don't forget to write!" Mollie said for the tenth time.

"I don't write so well," Jack said.

"That's why you are going to school," Mollie said. "Maybe they will have better luck getting you to study." She held out her arms and he stepped into her hug. He was taller than Mollie now. "I love you. Take care of your sister."

"Don't I always?" He hopped into the waiting stagecoach.

"It's time, Mollie," Charles warned.

Mollie turned to Casita. "Goodbye, my dear!"

Casita did not want to cry. The Army could take everything from her, but she would not give in to tears. She wouldn't let them see that they had beaten her again. She pulled a folded square of paper from her coat pocket. "This is for you," she said.

Mollie unfolded the drawing and saw a picture of herself,

sitting in the rocking chair in front of the fireplace. Her favorite flowered shawl was draped around her shoulders. Her hand rested on the top of her stomach; Casita had even drawn her wedding ring. Mollie's eyes were sleepy. Underneath, Casita had penciled in two words: "Mama waiting."

For once, Mollie didn't cry. Her dry eyes were clear and sad. "I'm not just waiting for the baby," she said, "I'm waiting for my other children to come home." She hugged Casita. "I love you. Take care of your brother."

Speaking past the lump in her throat, Casita tried to imitate Jack's happy-go-lucky farewell. "Don't I always?"

❖

The stagecoach lumbered to a stop in the great city of San Antonio, Texas. Jack and Casita were disappointed so far. They had heard of the enormous Spanish churches and the famous Alamo fort where the Indaa had lost so badly. But the train station was located on the outskirts of the town.

Charles helped Casita jump down. Her stiff legs nearly buckled underneath her as she shook the dust off her calico dress. Jack hopped out of the stagecoach. For him, the hardest part of the daylong trip had been being enclosed in the small coach. His suit was a dark grey and didn't show the dust from the journey. "Can we explore?" Jack asked.

Charles pulled out his pocket watch. "We don't have time. We'll wait in the station. The train leaves in two hours and four minutes." Charles snapped shut his timepiece.

"Your escort will find us there. He'll take you to Fort Hays in Kansas. A group of other children who are also going to Carlisle is gathering there."

Casita and Jack exchanged looks. Jack looked ready to meet any challenge. For him, three years at a boarding school was a small price to pay to ride a train. Casita was more like Mollie. What if the Army forgot about them? What if they got on the wrong train? Mollie had calculated the distances on the map before they had left. From Fort Clark to San Antonio was 140 miles. Fort Hays was almost 700 miles away from San Antonio. From Fort Hays to Carlisle was 1,300 miles more. Her mind couldn't imagine a distance that great. But Charles assured her that they would arrive in Carlisle in just a few days. Casita couldn't believe that was really possible.

Unaware of Casita's worries, Charles picked up her bag while Jack hoisted his on his shoulder and set off for the train depot. Charles's limp was worse after the long journey, but he still set a good pace. Casita wanted to stop and stare up at the tall two-story building. A steeple on top made it even higher. More coaches than she'd ever imagined in one place were jostling to find space in front of the station. Charles led them through the chaos as surely as if they were crossing the parade ground at Fort Clark.

Casita heard a loud rumbling. The ground beneath her feet shook. She froze. "Is it an earthquake?" she cried. She and Mollie had read of a terrible catastrophe in China where the earth had split apart, but Casita had never thought there could be one in Texas.

"It's just a streetcar," Charles said. "Look!" He pointed. A team of horses was pulling a metal house up the street. It glided along iron rails embedded in the road. "The streetcars bring people from here to the center of town."

"Can we go on one?" Jack asked.

"No," Charles said, pushing open the door to the depot. Casita had never seen such a room, with its high ceiling and high windows streaming in long rays of sunlight. Even the noise from all the people seemed to fly up high and bounce about. But it was the shops that caught Casita's attention. She couldn't believe how many there were. She saw signs for a barber, a pharmacy, a grocer, a bar, a restaurant, even a photography studio. *Everything a traveler might need*, she thought. With a start, she realized that Casita Smith was a traveler now, too. A large sign on the wall showed a train and proclaimed that the San Antonio railroad was "the shortest line to all points North, East, and West." Casita felt lightheaded; she was going both North and East.

"Before we meet your escort, there's something I want to do first." Charles led the children to the shop with a sign over the door that said "Photographer." Charles walked in and held the door behind him for Casita.

Casita took one step, then stopped before she cleared the doorway. "A photographer?" she said. "But . . ."

"I thought it would be a nice surprise for Mollie if I had your photograph taken."

"I will go," Jack said, pushing past Casita. He looked back at her. "Why do you look so afraid?"

"Don't you remember?" she whispered. He had been as nervous as she was when they first saw that picture of Mollie and Charles.

"That's just superstition," he said, sounding like Charles. "It's just a picture, and I want to see how it works."

Charles beamed and clapped Jack on the back. Reluctantly, Casita followed them inside.

The photographer came from behind a velvet curtain, surprised to find two Indian children. He brought them to a back room where there was an ornate table and chair. He seated Casita on the chair facing the camera and instructed Jack to stand next to her.

"You must sit perfectly still until I tell you it's all right to move. My plates have to develop."

The photographer lit enormous lamps that flooded the room with light. Ducking under the black cloth on the back of his camera, he said, "Ready?" His hand moved under the black cloth. Nothing happened.

"Don't move," he reminded them. Casita counted under her breath to fifteen. "That's it." The photographer emerged from the cloth. Jack ran up to him. "Can I see it?" he asked.

"This is only a plate with a picture embedded in it," he said. "I have to print it."

Charles laughed. "You'll have to wait to see it until you are home again."

"That will be years," Jack complained.

"When you return, you'll have grown up and we'll have to do another one."

Charles paid the photographer and they headed back into the train station, pushing their way through the waiting passengers. Casita stayed close to Charles, but Jack immediately disappeared.

"Where did Jack go?" she cried.

Charles chuckled. "Like any red-blooded American boy, he's looking at the trains." He pointed. There was a wide doorway on the far side of the depot. The sun was streaming down on the tracks. Jack was there, peering at the tracks, waiting for the train.

"Papa, where's the train?" he asked.

"It will be here soon enough."

In the distance, a long whistle blew. Jack ran down the paved platform to the edge of the depot so he would see the train first.

Like the streetcar, Casita heard the train before it appeared. Then a black gleaming machine rolled in, smoke belching from its smokestack. Jack ran alongside, whooping and pumping his fist.

"That's the motor that pulls the whole train," Charles shouted over the noise.

The motor was pulling a wagon with coal in it and four cars with windows and doors.

"How does it stop?" Casita asked, backing away.

Charles put his arm around her shoulders and kept her

next to him. "There are brakes. You'll see!" Sure enough, there was an awful squeal of metal scraping metal as the train began to lose speed. She clapped her hands over her ears, cringing as she waited for the crash. With a loud groan, the train came to a stop.

A conductor threw open the doors and passengers started getting out. No one seemed amazed that the train had stopped safely; they took it for granted. Casita wondered if she would ever be so calm about riding a train.

Jack was already examining the wheels that propelled the motor; they were almost as tall as he was. "Get back, Jack!" Casita ordered. "You'll be crushed."

"Don't be silly. It's not moving now," he said, waving away her fears. "When can we get on board?"

"In a minute," Charles promised. "Be patient." He never minded Jack's eagerness. Mollie said that Jack reminded Charles of himself as a young boy.

A man in a blue uniform like Charles's approached them. "Lieutenant Smith?" he asked. When Charles nodded, the soldier said he was Corporal Quinn, and Captain Carter had arranged for him to escort the children to Fort Hays.

"I have your tickets," Corporal Quinn said. "Let's get on board." They climbed into the first train car and Corporal Quinn showed them where they would sit. Casita had never seen leather so polished or so soft. Or polished lamps attached to a rounded ceiling. She couldn't believe that this small fancy house would really take them 700 miles.

"I have one more child to find. I'll be right back," Corporal Quinn said, hopping off the train.

Charles looked at his pocket watch. "It's time," he said. "I want you to make us proud at school."

"I will," Jack said, sticking out his hand for Charles to shake.

"Me, too," Casita said as she stepped into his gentle hug.

Blinking as if dust had gotten into his eyes, Charles said, "Good-bye." The train's whistle hooted again and he hurried off the train.

Left alone, Casita realized their escort hadn't returned. "Where is the Corporal?" she asked. "What if he doesn't come back? Charles has already left."

"You worry too much." Jack looked out the window at the thinning crowd on the platform. "There he is! And he's got another girl with him."

Casita pressed her face against the glass so she could see. The girl was younger than Jack, perhaps eight or nine years old. She wore a dark blue cotton camp dress, gathered at the waist and loose on top. Around her neck were red beads. Corporal Quinn held her hand, but she looked as if she wanted to take it back. There was something about her that reminded Casita of her cousin Juanita.

Corporal Quinn brought her on board and pointed to the seat next to Casita. The girl obediently sat down. To Casita, she looked like a tiny frightened doll.

"I'll be in the next car," Corporal Quinn said. "Fetch me if you need me. But only if it is important."

As soon as he was gone, Jack spoke in English. "What is your name?" He repeated the question in Ndé.

"I am Lenna," she replied. It was the first time Casita or Jack had heard their language spoken by someone else in three years. "I am Mescalero," she went on.

So Lenna wasn't really of their people, but she was Apache like they were. She was the same age Juanita would be now. The little girl was a stranger to Casita, but it felt like her family had returned to her.

Nde'

CHAPTER EIGHTEEN

"I AM CASITA." CASITA STARTED TO STICK HER HAND OUT, BUT then realized it was Indaa children who did that. Lenna would not understand. "This is my brother Jack. We are Cuelcahen Ndé."

As Lenna took in every detail of Casita's dress and boots and Jack's grey pants and shirt, Casita knew she was wondering about their clothes and their English.

"After a raid killed our family, we lived with a white family at Fort Clark for three years," Casita explained.

Lenna made an *O* with her mouth as she took in Casita's meaning. "My people live on a reservation in New Mexico," she said. "They are sending me to school to learn the ways of the Indaa."

Casita didn't know much about the Mescalero except that they were famous for the ways they could cook mescal and that they were allies of the Lipan.

"We are going to Carlisle, too," Casita said.

"What do you have to learn? You are already like the Indaa."

"Thank you," Jack said, beaming. Once he had started his life in the Army, he had embraced everything Indaa. Unlike Casita, he never had doubts. He never worried that he was betraying the Ndé. For that, Casita envied him.

The train jerked forward, throwing them back against their seats. Lenna cried out and clung to Casita's arm. Casita would have reassured her, but she was also scared by the train's power and noise. As the train picked up speed, Casita couldn't make out the scenes outside her window. It was like the world was spinning out of control and Casita couldn't make sense of it all.

"It's faster than any horse," Jack shouted over the noise. "I'm going to see the engine." As if he had been on a train dozens of times, Jack found it easy to adjust to its movements as he made his way through the car.

"He is very brave," Lenna said.

"He's not afraid," Casita corrected. "Even when he should be."

"I have a brother like that, too," Lenna said, smiling.

"Is he coming to the school, too?"

Lenna's face clouded. "He has to stay on the reservation. The Army only paid for one passage."

Casita rubbed Lenna's shoulders the way she used to

comfort Juanita. "Don't worry, you aren't alone."

❖

The trip to Fort Hays took over twenty hours. Casita and Lenna watched the passing scenery until their eyes were red and aching. When the train finally stopped at Fort Hays, Corporal Quinn hurried them off the train. "This isn't a regular stop on this line," he said. "They won't wait long."

No sooner had they climbed down from their car than the train whistled and pulled out. The land was so flat that Casita could see the horizon in every direction. It was colder here and the wind whipped their bodies. Corporal Quinn brought them inside the depot, telling them they would be met by the representative from the school.

Staying close to each other, they hurried into the plain, square building. They stopped short at the sight of a dozen Indian children sitting inside, their backs to the wall. Unlike Casita and Jack, they wore tribal clothes. Jack drew in his breath when he saw the feathered headdresses. Lenna slipped her hand into Casita's and whispered, "I've never seen Apache like them."

"That's because they aren't Apache," Casita replied.

A tall, grey-haired woman wearing spectacles approached them. "Corporal Quinn?" she asked.

"Yes, ma'am. Here are your children from San Antonio." He hurriedly signed a paper and left them without a word of farewell.

"I am Miss Mather," the woman said. She peered at a

stack of papers she had clipped to a board. "Lenna Cordova, Apache?"

Lenna nodded, too shy to speak.

Without looking at them, Miss Mather checked off Lenna's name on her list. Then she called "Casita Smith, Lipan." Check. "Jack Smith, Lipan." Check.

Casita thought perhaps she should explain that *Lipan* meant *Apache*, too, but was it important? Captain Carter had told them that tribes would not matter at the school, since the point was to teach them to be like white people.

"Do any of you understand English?" Miss Mather asked.

Jack spoke up first. "I speak English very well."

Miss Mather glanced up. She nodded with approval at his suit, now crumpled from travel. "You do speak well," she agreed.

"I learned at Fort Clark," he said, puffing up his chest.

"So you were with a military family?" Miss Mather's eyes rested on Jack's short hair with approval.

"Yes," Jack and Casita said together. Casita added, "I speak English, too. And I can read and write."

"Excellent," Miss Mather said, making a note. "Jack, I think you will do very well at Carlisle. Our train will arrive in an hour. In the trunk by the door, we have blankets and a lunch for each of you." When they didn't move immediately, she tapped the board with her pen. "Off with you, then."

Casita lifted her eyebrows. Was that all they were to be at Carlisle? Names on a list? Well, maybe not Jack. Miss Mather seemed to like him.

171

They had to pass the row of students to get to the blankets. Casita was disappointed to see that they were all boys. Casita had almost given up hope when she saw a girl her age on a bench in the corner. She sat alone and Casita was sure it was by her choice. She had the look of someone impatient with other people. Her dress made Casita envious. It was made of hide dyed deep blue, with a decorative fringe. An intricate pattern of elk's teeth and black beads was sewn across the bodice. She was beautiful, with skin that seemed to glow. But her lovely face was gaunt and her arms were very thin. While Casita watched, she had a coughing fit that left her breathless.

Jack wasted no time in getting to know the other boys. Some, although not many, spoke English, so he soon was able to tell Casita about all of them. The largest group was Sioux, but there were Arapaho and Kiowa children, too. They had been brought here from reservations by wagon and steamboat. They had been waiting for the train since the night before.

"Who is she?" Casita whispered to Jack.

"Her? Her name is Eyota. Her father is an important Lakota chief. He fought at Custer's Last Stand."

Casita and Jack eyed Eyota with even more interest. The Lakotas had wiped out the 7th Cavalry in one battle. Charles had been distraught, but Casita and Jack's reaction had been more complicated. They were an army family now—but for many years the news of such a defeat would have been celebrated among the Ndé.

"The Army wants Eyota to go to school to make sure

172

her father doesn't make any trouble," Jack said. "Like starting another war."

"She's a hostage." Casita's voice was flat. "No wonder she looks so cross."

"Maybe she looks cross because she's not a nice person," Jack said. "The Sioux boys don't like her. She acts like she's better than they are. But their fathers are chiefs, too."

A train whistle alerted them to the train's arrival, and they scurried to their feet. Jack grabbed his things and rushed to the platform. They might be the last arrivals, Casita thought, but Jack wanted to be the first one on the train. When she saw how the other boys admired Jack's bravery, she had to appreciate his tactics. He had just established himself as a leader.

Casita and Lenna trailed close behind. The Indian boys quickly followed, as if they couldn't be shown up by the courage of two girls.

"Can I sit by the window?" Lenna asked as they slid onto a long, cushioned seat.

"Of course," Casita said. It was an arrangement that would work very well for her. There was a vacant seat on her right and she hoped Eyota might sit there. Eyota might be cross, but she was the only other girl there. Mollie's suggestion that Casita could have friends her own age had found an echo in her heart. For too long she hadn't had anyone to confide her secrets to. What better way to become friends than to share a long voyage together?

Eyota was the last to board. She made her way down

the aisle, considering each vacant seat. When she came near Casita, Casita smiled at her and said, "You can sit here if you like." She held her breath, hoping the Sioux girl spoke English.

A wary expression on her face, Eyota sat down, her body stiff. So she did speak English. That was good, because Casita knew nothing of the Sioux or their language. The blue of Eyota's dress made her own dark grey skirt look drab, and Casita loved how the elk teeth made a clicking noise when the other girl moved. Now that she was so close to her, Casita heard the rasping of her breathing. Maybe it was just the cold or the dust at the station?

"My name is Casita," she said. "I'm Lipan Apache."

Grudgingly, as though she would prefer to spend the journey in silence, Eyota gave her name and tribe.

"I like your dress," Casita offered.

"I made it. My father said we should honor the school by wearing our best." That explained why the boys wore their finery. Eyota's gaze traveled down the length of Casita's Indaa dress. "That is a white woman's dress," Eyota said dismissively. "Are you sure you are Apache?"

"Of course I am," Casita said indignantly. "I was captured on a raid. I lived with a white family. They gave me this dress. But I am still Apache."

"Where I come from, if an Indian dresses like a white woman, smells like a white woman, and speaks their language, then she's not an Indian anymore. She is a traitor."

174

"I'm no traitor. Take that back. I'm as Indian as you are!" Casita almost shouted.

"You are nothing like me." Eyota stood up and moved to a different seat two rows up, just as the train lurched into motion. While the others moaned and hung onto their armrests as if they feared being sucked under the wheels of the locomotive, Eyota sat perfectly motionless. Either she wasn't scared at all, or she was petrified. From her calm manner, it was impossible to tell which.

While Lenna watched the passing fields, Casita kept her eyes on the back of Eyota's head, wondering that the Sioux girl took it for granted that you had to be either Indian or white. Just because Casita had chosen to live as Indaa didn't mean she wasn't Ndé. Casita was used to dealing with people like Caleb who didn't like her because she was Apache. But Eyota didn't like her because she seemed too white. Mollie had done her job well. What on earth was Casita going to do at a school that aimed to civilize Indians? Wasn't she white enough already?

Nde'

CHAPTER NINETEEN

It was midafternoon when Miss Mather announced they were approaching Carlisle. Casita and Lenna pressed their faces against the window, trying to make out any details about their new home. As she had for the whole journey, Eyota sat alone and acted indifferent.

The train slowed down and they saw the tracks went right through a main street of town. Casita could see brick banks and shops built into the bases of four-story stone buildings. They had been here a long time, she guessed. A horse and wagon were moving along the same path; the driver looked at Lenna as the train passed and waved. People were walking down the street with shopping baskets on their arms. They stopped to watch the train go by.

"What kind of place is this?" Lenna asked.

"A wealthy place," Casita answered.

The hiss and groan of the brakes signaled the train was

finally stopping. A small group of well-dressed men and women were waiting, stomping their feet on the frozen ground to keep warm. When they saw the children at the windows, they started to wave.

Miss Mather led the students off the train. As the children climbed down, the cold was the first to meet them. They huddled together, pulling their blankets tight around their shoulders.

"There's no snow," Jack said, disappointed.

Casita glanced up at the sky, heavy with dark clouds. "I'm sure there will be," she said. "Remember Mollie's stories. This is Pennsylvania." But she was disappointed, too. If it was going to be this cold, she thought, there should be snow.

A gentleman in a cavalry uniform advanced to meet Miss Mather. "Welcome home, Miss Mather!" he said for the benefit of the crowd. He didn't look like a stiff and clean-cut soldier. This man was pear-shaped with untidy white hair.

"Lieutenant Pratt, what a lovely welcome for our new students," she said, smiling warmly. She turned to the children, "This is the founder of our school, Lieutenant Pratt."

"I look forward to meeting the children," Lieutenant Pratt said. "But for now, it is rather cold. The good townspeople of Carlisle offered to transport our new arrivals to the school." He waved a hand toward two large wagons painted a bright cherry red. They were drawn by a team of six enormous horses that were much bigger than the cavalry horses Casita was

177

used to. Casita wouldn't even come up to their shoulders. Jack couldn't take his eyes off them.

"A hot meal is waiting for us at the school," Miss Mather said. "Hop in." Jack headed for the far wagon, but she stopped him. "Jack, come sit with me and Lieutenant Pratt. I'd like him to meet you."

Casita knew that Jack wanted to be with the horses, but he followed Miss Mather into the nearer wagon. Casita wondered, not for the first time, why Miss Mather liked Jack so much. On the train, she had asked him. He had grinned and said, "Don't you think Miss Mather is a good friend to have at the school?"

"Of course. But why you?"

"She said I remind her of a boy she used to know in St. Augustine."

Good for Jack, she thought. *He'll do well here.* She lifted Lenna into the wagon and climbed in after her.

Lenna huddled close to Casita. With two blankets around their shoulders, Casita and Lenna almost looked like one big bundle. "Don't leave me," Lenna whispered.

"I won't." Casita was happy to be Lenna's protector, especially since Jack had already replaced her with Miss Mather.

The trip was short, a mile, perhaps two. The horses clip-clopped on paved streets, effortlessly pulling the wagons away from the town center through a sleepy neighborhood of wooden houses. They went up a gradual slope with fields on either side and through an open gate. Miss Mather told Jack to close the gate behind them. As he jogged past their wagon, Jack waved to Casita and Lenna.

The wagons continued over a bridge that spanned a large creek, then past an open square, bordered by square buildings. Except for the white bandstand in the center, it reminded Casita of Fort Clark. Then she remembered that Captain Carter had said the school was in a former Army barracks. The wagons pulled up in front of a long white building at the corner of the square.

Lieutenant Pratt stood up in the wagon. "I've already asked Cook to have some hot soup waiting for you. You must all be hungry."

The children quickly crowded through the wide door. The room was lit by gas lamps and they saw ten or so rectangular tables and benches. Each table could seat six people. Three of them were already set with bowls of steaming soup, bread, and one apple for each of them. Tin cups had water. *It's the mess hall*, Casita thought. After three years on an Army base, she had never eaten in one.

"Boys at those tables, girls at that one," Miss Mather announced.

Eyota had to join Casita and Lenna at the girls' table, whether she wanted to or not.

"I'll have this one," Lenna said, sitting in front of the fullest bowl of soup.

The children wanted to eat as soon as they sat down, even those who were unfamiliar with the tin spoons, but Miss

179

Mather made them say grace first. "God is great. God is good. Let us thank Him for our food. Amen."

Casita and Jack knew the words; Mollie had taught them. They had had long discussions about what the Quakers believed and what the Ndé thought about God and gods. The other kids had no idea they were praying to an Indaa god, not an Indian one. But Casita saw that Eyota understood and did not like it.

The soup smelled like chicken, but it was thin. There were more vegetables than meat. But the hungry children were soon wiping the bowls with the bread to sop up every last bit.

Lenna slurped the last of her soup. "Do you think they will give us more?" she asked.

"You liked it?" Casita asked. She had learned to cook over the past three years, and she found the soup tasteless. "It wasn't very good."

"It's so much better than what we have at home," Lenna said. "There's not enough food at the reservation. That's why my father sent me here—they promised to feed me." She bit into her apple happily.

Casita couldn't help but laugh. The school wanted to civilize the Indians, which meant to change them completely. Some would resist, but others, like Lenna, would gladly submit for three square meals a day.

"What did she say?" Eyota asked in English, not understanding any Apache words.

"Lenna only came to school so she could eat."

A quick smile flitted across Eyota's lips. She handed her apple to Lenna, who gladly pocketed it. *Eyota's not as proud as she pretends to be*, Casita thought.

Lieutenant Pratt got up to speak after dinner.

"I know you have had a long journey, so I will be brief," he said. Casita thought she would like to draw the Lieutenant's face. She thought his eyes were like those of a giant eagle that could spot anything or see into the future. When Mother talked of keeping to the old ways, her eyes had looked like that, too. The resemblance made Casita wary of Lieutenant Pratt; how far would he go to get his way?

"Tonight you will be assigned your rooms in your dormitories. They are located across the square. We call it the 'quad.' Tomorrow we will place you in classes to learn English and mathematics and history. We will teach you a trade. You will go to church. Our rules are strict but fair. If you try hard, I will help you."

Casita shivered. This was a man who believed in his cause. She wondered what would happen if someone crossed him.

"You are coming to us as 'blanket children,' but when you leave Carlisle you will be Americans." He finished, "Your new life begins now."

As the translator explained the plan to the boys, Casita couldn't decide if Pratt's last words were a promise or a threat.

After dinner, Casita hoped to talk with Jack. But he was already first in line, marching out after Lieutenant Pratt without even looking back. She would find him later.

Casita, Eyota, and Lenna followed Miss Mather across

181

the quad to the girls' dormitory. It was another square white building. From a narrow porch that ran the length of the building, they stepped into a large cold room. The gaslights were turned down low, so Casita couldn't see into the corners. *Where were the other girls?* Casita wondered. There had to be more than just the three of them. A battered table and chairs in the corner hinted that others lived here, but it was eerily quiet.

A heavyset woman with a stack of papers and a stern face was waiting for them in a small office off the main room. Miss Mather introduced her as Miss Burgess. "She is one of your teachers. She also runs the print shop. Carlisle has its own newspaper, thanks to her." A small woodstove warmed the air, and Casita and the others crowded close, rubbing their hands.

A newspaper? Casita had practiced reading aloud from the papers from San Antonio and Chicago that arrived at Fort Clark weeks or even longer after they were printed. She wouldn't mind learning how to print the news.

Miss Burgess called out the girls' names one by one. "Lenna Cordova." Lenna raised her hand.

"How old are you, Lenna?" Miss Burgess asked. She held up her fingers. Understanding, Lenna held up both hands, all the fingers splayed out except for one.

"Nine. Very well. You will be in room 210."

Then it was Casita's turn. "Casita Smith," Miss Burgess read off her list.

Casita stepped forward. "Excuse me, but may I room with Lenna?" she asked.

"We don't allow children from the same tribe to stay together. We want you to stop speaking Indian." Mrs. Burgess checked the list. "It says that Lenna is Apache. What tribe are you?"

"Lipan," Casita answered, praying that Mrs. Burgess knew nothing about the number of tribes that might be called Apache.

"You're the first Lipan we have had. Where do you come from?" Mrs. Burgess asked.

"We came from Kansas," Casita began, but before she could explain she was from Texas, Mrs. Burgess was finished with her. "Very well. Casita Smith . . . Smith. That's not a good name. They'll think we have no imagination at all. Let's call you Roosevelt. Casita Roosevelt, you will be in room 210. That's on the second floor."

Casita stepped away and Eyota took her place. She confirmed her name and tribe. Yes, Eyota spoke English. Casita was only half listening. She was confused about the change to her last name. What made Roosevelt a better name than Smith? She had never heard that name before and didn't know why Mrs. Burgess had given it to her. Smith might not have been the name she was born to, but Mollie had liked it. How dare they change her last name without even asking? She turned back to Mrs. Burgess and Eyota. "Why did you change my name?"

"I beg your pardon?" Miss Burgess said.

"Why did you change my name?" Casita repeated. "What is wrong with Smith?"

183

"I am not accustomed to being questioned by students," Mrs. Burgess said coldly. "Roosevelt is a much better name." Casita hesitated, unsure how much she could say. But after all, what did her name really matter? Castro. Smith. Roosevelt. Did any of her names really define who she was?

Miss Burgess returned her attention to Eyota. "Since you are Sioux, you will be in room 210 with the other two girls."

Miss Burgess gathered up her papers and stood up. "It is almost time for you to go to bed. I've assigned Hazel to give you a tour of the building." She indicated an Indian girl who was waiting in the doorway. Finally, Casita thought, another girl. Hazel was Indian but wore a dark brown dress and brown leather boots that laced up. In fact, she and Casita wore practically the same clothes. She was a little older than Casita. "Hazel has strict instructions only to speak English. That is the rule here. I know that you two," she nodded to Casita and Eyota, "speak English, but Lenna doesn't. For tonight, you may translate for her."

Only tonight? Casita thought incredulously. She had learned her English over years, and Miss Burgess expected Lenna to manage in a day? She hoped the other expectations at Carlisle were more reasonable.

"Good night, girls," Miss Mather said. "I will meet you tomorrow at breakfast in the mess hall."

As soon as the teachers were gone, the girl introduced herself. "I am Hazel Dezay, Apache."

"What tribe?" Casita asked.

"I am Chiracahua from New Mexico."

184

Lenna recognized the words *Chiracahua* and *New Mexico*. She smiled widely and spoke Ndé. "My name is Lenna and I am Mescalero from New Mexico, too."

Hazel frowned. Speaking to Casita in English, she said sternly, "Please tell Lenna that I am not permitted to talk Indian."

Even though Lenna could not understand English, she knew that she had done something wrong.

Casita drew in a breath. She could sense that Eyota was also uncomfortable. Who could scold a child as sweet as Lenna? And what had this school done to Hazel, that she called her own language *talking Indian*?

Casita knelt down and gave Lenna a quick hug. "Let me take your coat," she said, unbuttoning Lenna's jacket. An apple rolled out of her pocket onto the floor. Lenna ran after it and held it tightly in both hands.

Hazel pursed her lips and shook her head. "We take our meals at the mess hall. It is forbidden to have food in the dormitory."

"Forbidden?" Eyota asked, her voice as cold as the air outside.

"Yes. Many things are forbidden here. You will see." She picked up two lit oil lamps, handing one to Eyota, then she led them out into the main room. "This is the common room. We are supposed to study here, but in the winter we prefer to study in our rooms."

"How many girls are there?" Casita asked.

"Including you? I think twenty. Most are my age, but

185

there are a few younger ones. There are a lot more boys than girls at Carlisle."

Eyota asked, "Where are they now?"

"It's almost time for lights out, so they are in their rooms getting ready for bed. We should hurry. We're not allowed out of our rooms after lights out." Moving stiffly, Hazel set off down a hall, dimly lit, to the rear of the building.

"This is the water closet," she said. Inhaling and then pinching her nose, she opened a small door. The small room was freezing and it reeked of excrement. A water tank hung high in the corner with a pipe that connected to a commode in the corner. A chain was attached to the tank and it hung within reach of the commode. Hazel explained how you pulled the chain and water would flush the bowl of the commode.

"Where does it go?" Casita asked.

"There's a tank outside."

"We may be savages," Eyota muttered, "but we don't do that inside our houses."

Hazel snorted as if she agreed.

She brought them up a narrow stairway to the second floor. As they passed rooms 200 through 209, Casita heard the murmur of girls' voices inside.

"Here is 210," Hazel said. "We don't have locks on the doors. The teachers inspect every Saturday."

Lenna rushed in the room; Eyota followed slowly. Casita was content to hang back. She wanted to talk with Hazel alone. "Is Carlisle a good place?" she asked.

"It is wonderful. I am learning to be Indaa and I could not be happier."

But Casita sensed that she was not telling the truth. Maybe she would confide to Casita if they spoke Ndé? "One Apache to another. How is it, truly?"

Hazel's head jerked, checking up and down the hall for listeners. "Do you really want to know?" she asked.

"Of course I do."

Hazel grabbed Casita's hand and pulled her into room 211. They were alone. She lit a lamp and closed the door.

"There are people listening everywhere," Hazel warned. "But we should be safe enough in here." She pulled up her skirt and turned away from Casita. Casita's eyes widened as she saw the ugly red marks across the back of Hazel's legs.

Swallowing hard, Casita asked, "What happened?"

"Miss Burgess beat me with her cane because she caught me stealing food."

"Do . . . do they do that a lot?" Casita stammered—and she could hear the fear in her voice. Among the Ndé, children were hardly ever beaten. Mollie the Quaker had not approved of corporal punishment either.

"It depends," Hazel admitted. "If they like you—if you do well in school or are helpful to the teachers—then you aren't disciplined. But they've never liked me. I'm a poor student and Miss Mather has heard me speaking Ndé too many times."

"So you've been beaten before?"

"Only once, when I didn't want to attend church."

Casita had never been to a church. Mollie told her how the Quakers liked to sit in a room and wait for God to speak to them. "What kind of church?"

"The Christian kind. First they take away our language and then our gods. If you want to pray to Usen, better do it where no one can hear."

"So there's nothing good here?" Casita asked. Three years could be a very long time.

Hazel leaned against the door and stared up at the ceiling. Finally she said, "Some of the teachers are kind. They want us to do well. But they still think to be an Indian is to be less than human. They will respect us when we look and talk and think just like them. I heard Lieutenant Pratt tell a visitor that he wanted to kill the Indian to save the man."

Casita had seen enough of Indians killed to last her whole life. She had escaped the guns of the 4th Cavalry at El Remolino. Would this Pratt kill Indians with schoolbooks and a strap? She felt as helpless as she had at Fort Clark. "Thank you for telling me," she said.

Hazel came close and whispered in Casita's ear. "There are girls here who try to win favor by reporting on the others. Don't trust anyone." She paused. "You could get me into trouble if you wanted to."

"You can depend on me," Casita promised.

Hazel brought her back to room 210. Lenna was bouncing on a white metal bed while Eyota stood at the small window.

"Get some sleep," Hazel said. "There are nightclothes for you in the chests. Later, we'll get you dresses."

"What kind of dresses?" Eyota asked from the window.

"Dresses like mine," Hazel said, holding out her dark skirt. "The boys have uniforms and we wear this."

Eyota studied Hazel's dress and turned back to the window. Casita suspected that Eyota would cause trouble and refuse to give up her buckskin dress.

"When the bugle plays 'Reveille' tomorrow morning, it will be time to wake up."

"'Reveille'?" Casita started to laugh. "For the last three years I've lived at an Army fort. I never thought I would wake up to 'Reveille' here, too."

"The bugle is our clock."

The bugling and discipline made sense, Casita thought, since Pratt was a military man.

"Punctuality is very important to Lieutenant Pratt and Miss Mather. If you want to make them happy, remember that wasting time, either yours or anyone else's, is a sin," Hazel said. "After 'Reveille,' you have half an hour before we leave for the mess hall. Good night." She slipped out the door.

"Where did you go, Casita?" Lenna asked.

"Never mind," Casita said, looking round the room. Her voice echoed and Casita glanced up to see the ceiling was high. There were three beds against the walls and a table and chairs in the center of the room. Shelves were attached to

189

one wall. Lenna and Eyota's knapsacks were on two of the beds. Casita went to the third.

"I have a chest," Lenna said, pulling a small chest out from under the bed.

"You can put all your treasures there," Casita said.

Lenna's face fell. "But I don't have any treasures."

Her words brought Casita back to a time when Juanita had made the same complaint. Casita had taken her to the river to find pretty stones. She could help Lenna, too. "I'll share one of mine," she offered. Rummaging through her knapsack, she found her shell necklace tucked inside her rolled-up needlepoint. Casita's hand hovered between the two before she chose the embroidery. "You can take this for now."

"It's beautiful," Lenna said. "Did you make it?"

"I did," Casita said, thinking of all those hours on the porch at home. Mollie had despaired of teaching her, but Casita had finally learned the knack of using the thin needle. "You can keep it until you find a treasure of your own."

Casita knelt on the floor to unpack her knapsack, placing everything just so in the chest. Her thoughts were jumbled: the needlepoint was a reminder of a happy life only just taken from her. The necklace was from a past that she had left behind. But in that moment, she had chosen to keep the necklace. Mollie had been right: a reminder of her Ndé past was important here.

Outside there came the mournful sound of "Taps." Eyota peered outside.

"It's the way the Army says it is time to sleep," Casita said. She translated for Lenna's benefit.

"Can't they see when it gets dark?" Eyota asked.

Casita smiled, remembering her discussion with Charles.

Eyota opened her chest. She lifted up the nightgown and examined it suspiciously. Rubbing the fabric against her cheek, she sneezed. "I don't need their clothes," she said, replacing the nightgown in the chest. She removed her moccasins and slipped under the covers.

"Is she going to wear her dress to bed?" Lenna asked.

"If she does, it is her choice." But Casita remembered her talk with Hazel. Did they really have any choices here? She doubted Eyota would be able to wear her colorful dress for long.

Casita helped Lenna into the nightgown, showing her how to use the buttons at the neck. Lenna loved her new nightgown. She danced around the room, letting it billow around her ankles. Casita unbuttoned her own dress and laid it over the metal bed frame. She massaged her skull with her fingertips; she was suddenly so tired. "How did you get that scar?" Lenna asked.

It was the first time anyone had ever asked her. Everyone at Fort Clark, including Mollie, had assumed it was a wound from the raid. Even Jack hadn't thought to ask more.

"It happened a long time ago," she said, pulling the nightgown over her head. "I don't want to talk about it."

She blew out the lamp.

Nde'

CHAPTER TWENTY

THE NEXT MORNING THEY WERE ALL STILL ASLEEP WHEN "REVEILLE" sounded. Eyota sat bolt upright, her eyes darting about the room.

"It's all right," Casita said. "Remember, they play it when it's time to get up."

"Every day?" Eyota asked, dismayed.

Casita shook Lenna, who was still sleeping soundly, a little snore escaping from her mouth. "Wake up! Hazel said breakfast will be in half an hour. We should get ready." She put on her spare dress, a pale green one.

Eyota looked as though she hadn't slept. Her eyes were red and she couldn't keep from coughing. She smoothed the hide of her blue dress with her fingertips. Today she didn't seem as proud as she had before. She seemed alone and scared. Maybe, Casita thought, she needed a friend.

She pulled a chair up to Eyota's bed and asked gently, "Tell me about your dress."

Eyota answered simply, "I made this dress with my mother. We were planning another one when the Army took me away."

Eyota's words were like a punch to Casita's stomach. Her mother, too, had planned a dress for Casita. A dress whose ashes had long since blown away in Mexico.

In a low voice, so low that Casita didn't know if she was supposed to hear it, Eyota said, "I hate it here. I want to go home."

"The Indaa word is *homesick*," Casita said quietly. "You are sick for home." She stood up. "We should get ready."

Downstairs, twenty girls waited for them. The older girls ignored them, except for Hazel, who said good morning. Miss Burgess was standing there, holding up a tiny clock that hung around her neck. "Punctuality is next to godliness, girls." She blew a whistle and they marched across the quad to the mess hall.

"We march everywhere," Hazel said without moving her lips. "They think it's good discipline for us."

"If I wanted to march," Casita muttered to Hazel, "I would have stayed at Fort Clark." Charles had once told her that the soldiers practiced marching together so they would all think as one unit.

At breakfast, Casita saw that Hazel hadn't exaggerated the number of boys; there must have been at least 150. It was like Fort Clark in that, too—Mollie had always complained about how few women there were to talk to. The boys wore uniforms and had short hair. It was easy to find the Indians who had traveled with them, with their long hair and their colorful clothes. It wasn't so simple to find Jack. But when she did, he looked right at home. His clothes weren't all that different from the uniforms. And hadn't he gotten along with the soldiers at the fort?

Lieutenant Pratt walked in, followed by Miss Mather, who seemed well rested and full of energy. One would never guess she had just come halfway across the country the day before. They stopped to chat with Jack.

"Is that your brother?" Hazel asked across the table. When Casita nodded, she said, "If Miss Mather likes him, he'll have no trouble at all."

After Lieutenant Pratt said grace, they ate their porridge. Then Miss Mather stood up to make several announcements. There was going to be a special outing for the oldest boys in town. A reverend was coming to be the special guest at Bible study this evening. The ice on the pond was not yet strong enough for skating.

"And the new students will have their photographs taken today. I will bring you to the art studio immediately after our meal."

A special space just for making art? Casita was eager to see it and get her hands on some paper and pens. She could draw thousands of pictures of all the new people and places she'd seen since Fort Clark.

Before they left, Casita found Jack. "How are you, Brother?" she asked. She didn't need to break any rules, because his English was quite good. "I've been worried about you."

"Why?" he asked. "I love it here. I haven't had friends my own age for a long time."

Jack's last friends had been the boys in the Seminole camp. She understood why he seemed so happy now.

"Are you settling in?" he asked.

"I don't know," she answered honestly. "Last night one of the girls told me about being beaten just for taking some food. And being punished because she spoke her own language."

"She sounds like a troublemaker," Jack warned. "Didn't you hear Lieutenant Pratt? We will learn faster and better if we only speak English. And his rules are to protect us all—if everyone stole food, there wouldn't be anything to eat."

Casita felt sick. How had Jack become such a supporter of Carlisle overnight? How did Pratt do it? In the distance she heard a bugle. Here it wouldn't be the signal for drills or fatigue—it was probably for class. Pratt used Army discipline to make his school work. Jack hadn't really become a convert overnight. He had been absorbing the Army's lessons all along, from Charles and from Corporal Brody in the stables.

The workshops were behind the boys' dormitory. There were four long buildings; Casita tried to count the windows of each one and stopped when she reached fifteen. Jack abandoned her to run with the other new boys. Miss Mather told them that they would work in one of these buildings depending on their skills. For the boys, there was tin-making, carpentry, printmaking, shoemaking, or blacksmithing. For the girls, there was dressmaking and the kitchens.

The art studio was tucked behind the woodworking shop and it was everything Casita had hoped. A dozen easels stood around the room and the students' works-in-progress were there for her to see. They had written their names on the bottoms of the pictures. She felt like she was actually meeting the students. The current task was to draw a bowl of fruit that was placed on a table in the center of the room. She looked from Joshua Lozen's picture to the fruit and back again. Somehow, Joshua had made it so that the fruit in front seemed closer in his picture than the fruit in back. Casita had no idea how he did that.

Miss Mather saw her interest and said, "We have two art instructors who come each week."

"I would like that more than anything." The words came easily to Casita. Maybe this was how Pratt won over his children; he offered them opportunities to do what they loved best.

A photographer had set up a backdrop of a fanciful landscape behind a chair and table. Miss Mather called him Mr. Choate and said he was from the town of Carlisle. He would take their picture today and then again in a few months.

Lenna's hand crept into Casita's. "Is it true that the camera will take our souls?" she asked in a whisper.

196

"No," Casita assured her. "Jack and I had our picture taken in San Antonio and we are fine."

To her surprise, Miss Mather wanted to photograph her and Jack together. "We like to keep families together for our records," she explained.

When he saw them, Mr. Choate asked Miss Mather, "Is this the before or after?"

"Before," she answered.

He lifted his eyebrows. "They came here already looking like that? They're making it easy for you." Casita wondered what they were talking about. But she had no one to ask before Mr. Choate seated her on a stool and positioned Jack standing next to her. "Ready, children?" Mr. Choate called.

This time Casita was more relaxed than the first time she was photographed. She even leaned on a table with her arms crossed. While she waited, she wondered about the others and why the school wanted pictures of them in their buckskins and beads. Wasn't the whole point to take away any signs of being Indian?

Once Mr. Choate released her and Jack, she wandered about the art room. Near the entrance, she found a series of framed photographs hanging on the wall in pairs. She found Hazel, wearing a camp dress and a colorful patterned blanket around her shoulders. Her hair was loose and she wore a headband with intricate beading that Casita recognized as Chiracahuan. In the next picture, Hazel wore her dark dress and had her hair neatly pulled back. She didn't look like an

Apache anymore: she even looked paler. *Ah*, thought Casita, *that is the key. They want before and after. Savage and Civilized.* Casita wondered if her "after" picture would show any difference.

She returned to the photographer. It was Eyota's turn. She looked proud and strong in her blue dress. Casita tried to picture what she might look like in a few months. It was hard to imagine that Eyota would let the school change her much. Next it was Lenna's turn. She looked so small. Even Miss Mather seemed to soften when she saw how frightened Lenna was of the camera. She sat with her until the picture was taken.

Holding Lenna's hand, Miss Mather beckoned to Casita and Eyota. "I know you are eager to start classes, but first we have a few administrative tasks." She brought the three girls to the infirmary, a tiny square stone building at the edge of the quad. The infirmary contained one large room, cut in half by a screen. It smelled of bleach, reminding Casita of the hospital at Fort Clark. Miss Burgess sat at a desk, filing papers into folders. She introduced them to a tall, stooped man named Dr. Granger.

"I am just going to take some measurements and see if you are healthy," he said. "Who is first?"

"Casita Roosevelt," Miss Burgess announced. She gave Casita a hard look, as if she expected her to complain about her last name again.

Dr. Granger and Miss Burgess brought her behind the screen. He put her on a scale while Miss Burgess recorded her weight and height. Next, he wrapped a long cloth measuring tape around her chest and had her inhale deeply. If that wasn't bad enough, then he unbuttoned her dress. He placed a flat metal disk against her bare skin. Casita saw that it attached to tubes that went into his ears.

"Casita, breathe in. Breathe out." The doctor paused. "What's this?" He touched the scars on her shoulder. "She has some deep scars on her shoulder and neck." Without asking, he lifted up her hair. "And her head. I'd guess they are a few years old." Miss Burgess took down every detail. He stepped back to see Casita's face. "How did you get those scars?" he asked.

Casita hesitated. Should she tell them the truth? It probably wasn't a good idea to lie on her first day. Since hearing what Hazel had experienced, Casita wanted to be a good student. After all, what did it matter? Her mother had tried to kill her, but Mother was dead now.

"My mother hit me with a rock," she said quietly. "Three times."

Casita could only hear the scratching of Miss Burgess's pen.

"Why?" Dr. Granger asked.

"The soldiers were attacking our village. She did not want me to be taken prisoner." Such a simple explanation for a complicated thing. Mother had loved her children, and she had died to protect them.

"She tried to kill you?" Miss Burgess demanded. "Doctor, I have to say that I can still be shocked by what these people will do."

199

"It will make a good story for that newspaper of yours," Dr. Granger said.

"You've read it, Doctor?" Miss Burgess blushed.

"I think it is excellent. Our donors need to know the good we are doing here. Look at this poor girl. She's much safer with us. Her own mother tried to kill her. If we can keep her away from her people, we can save her."

A thousand memories flashed in Casita's mind. Her mother teaching her to cook. Her mother's cool hand on her brow when she was sick. Casita perched high on the rocks watching her mother clean a hide for Casita's ceremony. She had been angry with her mother for so long. But did one desperate act really erase all the love and care that came before? Was she better off at the Carlisle School than she had been in El Remolino?

The doctor dismissed her and she walked out to the waiting area.

"What did they do to you?" Eyota asked. Before Casita could reassure her, Miss Burgess came to collect her.

"Does it hurt?" Lenna asked.

"Of course not," Casita said. She sat down and began to explain everything to Lenna, when they heard Eyota shouting.

"Stay away from me." There was a scuffle and a slapping sound.

Casita hurried behind the screen to see Eyota standing like a trapped animal in the corner.

"Do not touch me," Eyota cried.

"You will do as we say," Miss Burgess said angrily.

Dr. Granger was moving toward Eyota with his measuring tape and listening device.

"Doctor," Casita said urgently. "Eyota speaks excellent English. Maybe if you explain to her what you are doing . . . I am sure she will cooperate."

Glancing at Miss Burgess's red face, he said, "I suppose it can't hurt. Young lady, I am going to listen to your heart with my stethoscope."

"It doesn't hurt," Casita assured Eyota.

The doctor listened. "Breathe in. Breathe out." He looked concerned. "She seems to have some congestion in her lungs. Make a note, Miss Burgess."

Casita waited with Lenna during her examination, too.

Afterwards, Miss Burgess took Casita aside. "You were very helpful today."

"Thank you, ma'am," she answered. "I want to do well here." Maybe Miss Burgess would forget how Casita had challenged her the night before if Casita was humble enough now?

"If you continue this way, you have a bright future at Carlisle," Miss Burgess said, smiling kindly.

Which Miss Burgess was the real one? The one who beat Hazel or this one, who handed out promises and kindness? Last night, Casita had protested angrily when her name was changed. Today, she had helped keep Eyota from making trouble. She had told herself she was rescuing Eyota, but wasn't Casita also making sure that the authorities liked her?

Was this how Carlisle broke the Indian children? By

alternating kindness with threats? Scare one with a belt but offer another the chance to draw? Frightened children were easy to mold into Pratt's idea of a civilized Indian. But Casita saw through their tactics. If she became "civilized" it would be because she chose to, not because they tricked her.

Nde'

CHAPTER TWENTY-ONE

Miss Burgess brought Lenna to a class where the students would learn English, but Casita and Eyota were sent to Miss Mather. Seated at her tidy desk, Miss Mather explained how their education at Carlisle would proceed.

"You have classes in the morning and work in the afternoon," she said. "We sort the students by their abilities. Casita, I think your brother said you read and write English?"

Casita nodded, distracted by a strange wailing noise outside. Like hyenas howling in the desert.

Miss Mather made a note in Casita's folder, then turned to Eyota. "What about you? Did you go to the school at the reservation?"

"Yes," Eyota said, "I can read a little."

"For now, I will put Casita in the sixth grade class, and Eyota, you are in the third grade."

"Why is she so much higher than me?" Eyota asked, bristling.

"Because writing is a difficult skill to master," Miss Mather said with a frown.

"If you like," Casita offered, "I could help you."

The noise outside grew even louder.

"What on earth?" Miss Mather said, hurrying to the window and opening the sash.

Casita and Eyota exchanged glances.

"What is it?" Eyota whispered. Casita raised her shoulders.

Miss Mather started to chuckle. "Never mind. It's just the new boys."

Jack? "What's happening to them?" Casita asked.

"Nothing. The barber has arrived to cut their hair." Casita and Eyota stared at her, horrified. "Lieutenant Pratt thinks that long hair is just too Indian."

"That is because a boy's hair is like . . . himself," Eyota cried.

To an Indaa, it might seem like a simple haircut, Casita thought, but to a Ndé it was the worst cruelty. No wonder the boys were crying. Casita touched her own braid, and a horrible thought occurred to her. "Will you cut our hair, too?"

"No," Miss Mather assured them. "I persuaded Lieutenant Pratt that a girl's best feature is her long hair, whether she is Indian or white."

Closing the window, Miss Mather returned to her desk. "The next thing is your names."

"What about our names?" Casita asked. She had already

lost *Smith* the night before. Did they want to take her first name, too?

"All of our students take a white first name," Miss Mather said. "We'd like to change all the Indian last names, too, but it is too difficult for our recordkeeping."

Casita frowned, remembering how Miss Burgess had changed her name from Smith to Roosevelt for no reason at all. Maybe the school changed their names to prove to the students that they were powerless.

"First our hair, now our names," Eyota grumbled. "Do you leave us anything?"

Miss Mather narrowed her eyes. "You just have to trust that we know best."

"*Casita* is a Spanish name," Casita said quickly.

"It's very pretty. It doesn't sound Indian at all. You can keep it if you like. But *Eyota* is definitely too Indian."

"Among my people, it means 'the great one,'" Eyota said.

"Exactly," Miss Mather said. "Not precisely the message we want to send, especially given your father's situation. He is counting on you to be obedient. Do you have a name you like?"

"Eyota."

"A white girl's name," Miss Mather said. "What about Eunice? That sounds like Eyota."

"No it doesn't," Eyota said boldly.

"Eunice Flying Hawk," Miss Mather said, writing it down. "Very well. Now we need to pick your workshop in the afternoon. We want you to learn a skill so that when you are finished with Carlisle you can find meaningful work." Miss Mather craned her neck to see Eyota's dress. "This is very detailed work. Did you make it yourself?"

Eyota nodded.

"Then I think I will place you with the seamstresses. They make all the uniforms. You can learn to use a sewing machine."

Brightening in spite of herself, Eyota said, "I've heard about sewing machines."

"They are very useful," Miss Mather said, pleased with her progress. She turned to Casita. "Now, Casita, do you like to sew?"

"I am not very good," Casita said quickly. "Is there a workshop for art?"

"I'm afraid not. Art is a class, not a trade."

"What about the newspaper?"

Miss Mather beamed. "I think that could be arranged. Miss Burgess has asked for some girls. It seems the boys have trouble using the small types for the letterpress. Class has just started, so I will bring you to your rooms now." Eyota and Casita followed her out into the hall. "Oh, Eunice, our students must wear appropriate clothes. We will issue you both uniforms this afternoon."

"You want to take my dress?" Eyota's face was pale.

"Don't worry. You can make yourself a new one. One that suits your life at Carlisle better."

"I won't do it," Eyota insisted.

"You don't have a choice, my dear."

206

Casita realized that Miss Mather had only let Eyota keep her dress for the photograph. "It's only a dress," Casita whispered to Eyota. She was bound to lose more than a dress at Carlisle. The school was robbing the students of their pasts as easily as the Army had taken all their land. Casita decided that she would never use the name *Eunice*. It might seem like a small thing, but names were important. Too important to give up just because the school thought they were too Indian.

❖

Casita worried all day about Eyota, but she didn't have a chance to talk to her until they were back in their room. Even then, she didn't want to ruin Lenna's night. Lenna was delighted with her new friends and her new name.

"There was a board with names. I didn't know what any of them meant. The teacher told me to just pick one. So now I'm Nelly. You have to teach me how to write it," she told Casita.

Feeling like a big sister, Casita folded back the blanket on Nelly's bed. "Time for sleeping."

Nelly leapt into bed and was asleep within a few minutes.

Eyota lay on her bed, staring at the ceiling.

"It was a hard day," Casita said.

There was no answer.

"My teacher gave me a pen and ink and paper. I'm going to write to my family and tell them about the school. If you want to write to your father, I could help."

Turning her head to the wall, Eyota said, "Didn't you

hear her mention my father's situation? The Army sent me here so he would not start a war. If I tell him I am unhappy, he might do something bad and the Army could send him to prison. I can't write him."

Casita had thought Eyota's father had to be good because the government had his daughter. But now she saw that Eyota had to be good to protect him. She missed Mollie terribly, and she was grateful that there was nothing to keep her from writing home.

She dipped her pen in the inkwell and began to write.

❖

March 5, 1880
Dear Mama,
I have been at the school for a few days now. We can write a letter home every two weeks. I give it to Miss Mather (she is the second in command at the school) and she posts it for us.

Jack is well. He is already a favorite of Miss Mather's. The boys are organized like they are in the Army. Even though Jack is young, he thinks he will be a captain soon. They practice marching and drill with rifles once a day in the quad. If the weather is bad, they use the gymnasium. The girls don't have to learn the rifle, but we march all the time. It reminds me of the soldiers at home, so I do not mind too much.

One of the first things they do here is give us a new

name. They let me keep Casita *because it did not sound too Indian. But they changed my last name to* Roosevelt. *I don't know why.*

I am studying in a real classroom, which is much bigger than the parlor in our house. There are desks and blackboards. My teacher, Miss Anthony, is strict but she is kind. She thinks you did a good job teaching me geography. In the afternoon I work in the print shop.

Each week our rooms are inspected for cleanliness and to make sure we don't have any Indian things that are forbidden. Luckily I know how to keep things spick and span. We are allowed to have small keepsakes from home, but not ones that are too powerful, like a knife or an eagle feather.

I share a room with two girls. There's Nelly, who is a Mescalero Apache. She is younger than me and very sweet. She reminds me of my cousin Juanita and depends on me, and I like that. I am teaching her English.

The other girl in my room is Sioux and she is named Eyota. They try to call her Eunice but she hates it. I won't call her that. She is very homesick. She has a bad cough and I worry about her. The doctor says it is not serious, but he doesn't hear her at night when she cannot sleep.

I think of you every day, from "Reveille" to "Taps." Write soon and tell me about the baby.

Love, Casita

❖

March 19, 1880

Dear Mama,

It has been two weeks since my last letter. I miss you and Charles very much and wish you would write.

My teachers are pleased with me. Even though I am the youngest in my class, I know English the best. Sometimes when we study history, we get angry. The Indians are always bad in the history book. The writers of the book never talk about all the broken treaties or the land the United States stole.

Last week the art teacher finally came. His name is Professor Little (He is really called that! And the school thinks we need new names!). He asked us to draw scenes from home. I drew a picture of you and Charles. He said I am very good, but I must learn something called "perspective." Next week I must draw a bowl of fruit. Usually I draw things I care about, but I will do what Professor Little tells me.

In the printing workshop I have learned how to set type. It is very boring but I have small hands and I am better at the task than the boys are. The boys are good at taking the long rolls of paper and feeding them through the printing machine. The machine is loud and fast. I am afraid I will catch my sleeve or my skirt on the roller.

In the afternoons Jack works at the blacksmithing workshop. He likes being near the huge draft horses and

the fire. I do not talk to him often. He lives in the boys'
dormitory and he is in a different class than me. If he
wanted to, he could visit me in the common room of the
girls' dormitory, but so far he has not.

The rules are very strict here about speaking English.
Every Saturday night after dinner, Lieutenant Pratt
does a roll call and we have to answer "Indian" or "No
Indian." If we answer "Indian," it means we spoke our
own language that week. Last Saturday Eyota said
"Indian" and didn't care when Lieutenant Pratt scolded
her. Eyota speaks English almost as well as I do, so I
think this is her way to keep something of herself. Miss
Burgess said if it happens again, she will hit her with
the cane.

Eyota is still ill. Is it possible to die from
homesickness? At first she refused to write to her people
and ask to come home. But when she heard the Sioux
have been cooperating with the Army, she decided to write
to her father. Maybe he can bring her home now.

Yesterday we went ice skating. There is a creek that
runs behind the school and they dam it up. Dam is not
a bad word if I mean they block the water to make a
pond. The weather has been cold and the pond is finally
frozen. I did not like skating. I like to keep my feet on
the ground, not sliding away from me. Charles was right
when he said that Jack would be good at it. After just
a few minutes he was skating very fast. It was a lucky
thing, too, because my friend Nelly slid into some reeds

sticking up out of the ice. They must have made the ice weak, because it began to crack. She screamed for help, but the teachers were on the other side of the pond. Jack raced to rescue her. And now Jack is a hero. Miss Mather wants us to write an article about him for the newspaper, but I think he has already been praised too much. My teacher says the expression is "he has a big head." But I am very glad Nelly did not drown in the cold water.

Every time it snows, I think of you. Please, please write. I want to hear about the baby. I love you.

Casita

❖

April 7, 1880
Dear Mama,

Why do you not write? It has been almost six weeks since I came to Carlisle. The baby must be here. Perhaps you are too busy. But when you have a moment, please write to me.

Some new students arrived this week. One of them is from Alaska! But he could not find it on a map during geography. To be fair, I don't think he had ever used a map or even seen one before.

Have I mentioned the food? It is not very good. The school says it doesn't have enough money to buy better food. We hardly ever have meat and I am often still hungry after dinner. You always told me that what we ate would keep us healthy. I am afraid that the food is making Eyota even sicker. She has not heard from her family yet.

We are about to publish the second edition of the newspaper. The first one came out before I arrived. I set the type for the articles, so I know before anyone else what will be printed. Miss Burgess writes most of the stories but someday I might write one, too. Everything Miss Burgess writes is true, but she doesn't tell every story. There is nothing about the boys who cried for a full night after their hair was cut. Or about the two girls who were so unhappy they tried to burn down the girls' dormitory. Don't worry—they did not succeed and now they are in the jail in town. Or the children who get sick. Many of us are sick. I think it must be the cold and wet weather. She did write about one boy who died, but he already had a bad disease when he came. There will be a story about me in it but I haven't seen it yet. The paper is called Eadle Keahtah Toh, *which is Sioux for* The Morning Star. *Miss Burgess said they might change the name to something that is not Indian.*

Lieutenant Pratt has us send the newspaper to more than 2,000 people around the country. Some are politicians in Washington who give the school money. Some are families on the reservations, so they can see how good the school is. Miss Burgess said we can send you a copy. I will help address some of the newspapers because I have fine handwriting. I will make sure I address your copy myself.

We also print postcards. One of the postcards has my

213

picture on it. I will ask Miss Burgess for one so I can send it to you. Maybe that will help you remember to write. Please give my love to Charles. I miss you both.

Casita

❖

April 30, 1880
Dear Mama,
I decided not to send you the newspaper after all. I did not like what they said about me. I told them the truth, but they made it sound like my mother was a terrible person.

I hope you are well. I am sure I will receive a letter from you soon. I think of you and home all the time. Charles will be happy that Jack has become a bugler here. We still play our game; I can almost always get dressed before he plays "Reveille."

Yesterday a Quaker lady came to visit the school. She wants the school to have a band and she will give us the instruments. Miss Mather says the band will play in parades all over the country. Jack is very excited because he wants to learn to play the tuba. Maybe one day he can come back to Fort Clark and be in the 4th Cavalry Marching Band. Like father, like son.

Our days are always the same. We march to meals, then class, then lunch, then work, then dinner. After 7:00 pm we cannot leave the dormitories. There are common rooms where we can talk (in English) or study.

I like studying in my room best. I have put all my drawings on the wall, just like I did at home. I hope you have left my pictures there, because when I come home I want to see how much I've improved.

The schoolwork is getting harder, especially the math. My teacher says I don't try hard enough. That made me sad because you worked so hard to teach me. I am sorry. If only I could hear from you or Charles, I would study harder.

Casita

❖

May 13, 1880
Dear Mama,
I wish I could see you and ask for your advice now. Jack came to visit me yesterday. He told me that Miss Mather wants to adopt him and make him her son. She is going to Florida next year and wants to take him with her. I shouted at him and told him that he was already someone's son. But he said he wants to go with her. His new name is Jack Mather. Florida is so far from here that I'm afraid I'll never see him again.

After everything we have been through, I thought Jack and I would always be together. Of all the things the school has already taken from us, I didn't expect them to take Jack, too. I told him to write to you and explain. Maybe you can make him change his mind.

My friend Nelly is doing very well. She loves the

*school. Back on her reservation, she did not have enough
to eat. Here she grows fat.*

*I wish I could say the same for Eyota. After writing
two letters home, she has heard nothing. I helped her
write the letters and the envelopes, so I know they were
addressed correctly. I told Miss Mather that I was scared
for her. She said the mail could be unreliable and she
would write to the Sioux reservation herself. I hope we
hear soon. I wish you were here, Mama, to take care
of her.*

*Maybe the mail has been unreliable and that is why
I haven't received a letter. I hope you and Charles and
the baby are well. Maybe now that you have a baby, you
don't want your Lipan children any more. No matter
what, I will always love you.*

Casita

Nde'

CHAPTER TWENTY-TWO

THE CALENDAR SAID IT WAS MAY. SPRING IN PENNSYLVANIA WAS full of life and color, a treat for eyes used to the desert. The trees were covered with a fur of light green growth and the bushes next to the mess hall were budding with yellow flowers. Mrs. Pratt's little garden had sprouted a batch of tulips that looked like jewels. Casita was happy to volunteer for any errand that brought her outside in the sunshine.

The next edition of the newspaper was being printed today. Miss Burgess had asked her to deliver a copy to Miss Mather, but when Casita got to Miss Mather's office, she wasn't there. Casita entered the office and proudly placed the paper in the center of her desk, shifting the folders that were there to one side. When she did, one of the folders slipped to the floor. Casita knelt to retrieve it and paused. . . . Eyota's name was on the folder.

Did Miss Mather have it out because Eyota was in

trouble? Casita knew Eyota refused to study and often argued with her teachers. Only her poor health had kept her from being punished. Casita couldn't resist; she had to know so she could warn her friend. She went to the door and checked that the hallway was deserted. Then she darted back to the desk and opened the folder. There was a medical form and a report card. That was expected; every student had one. But underneath these official pieces of paper were several letters addressed to Chief Flying Hawk at the reservation. Casita recognized Eyota's labored handwriting. The letters to her father, each more desperate than the last, had never been sent. Miss Mather had kept them. No wonder Eyota's people had never responded. Even worse, Miss Mather had lied to Casita when she'd said the letters had gone astray. Why would she do that?

Eyota had told Casita that the largest number of students at Carlisle came from the Sioux reservations, because the Army wanted the children of the chiefs far from their families. In return, the Army helped Lieutenant Pratt raise funds for the school. Maybe Pratt didn't want Eyota's father to know that she was ill and unhappy. Would they really let Eyota's heart break just to keep their reputation with the Sioux chiefs? Casita feared the answer was yes.

She took Eyota's last letter and shoved it in her skirt pocket. If the school could hide the students' letters, they could do anything. But what about Casita's letters home? Maybe Mollie had written to her and Miss Mather had kept her letters from Casita. Was there any reason for her to do that?

Yes. Miss Mather wanted to adopt Jack. How much easier it would be for her if Jack were cut off from the Smiths. Miss Mather wouldn't care that Casita was cut off too, especially if she had read Casita's letters and knew that Casita had tried to talk Jack out of the adoption.

She had to know for certain if Miss Mather had betrayed her like she had Eyota. There was a cabinet in the corner of the room with the students' files. She pulled out the first drawer. The files were sorted alphabetically by last name. Would Miss Mather use Smith or Roosevelt? Her fingers were trembling as she checked each folder. This cabinet was A–F anyway. She closed it harder than she meant, and the slamming noise echoed in the room. The next drawer was G–P. The third one should have hers.

There were voices in the hall. If Miss Mather caught her going through the files, Casita would surely be caned. She tiptoed to the door and peered out. No one. She might not get another chance at Miss Mather's files. She had to do it now. She opened the third drawer. Racine. Rankin. Red Deer. Red Eye. Red Horse. Red Star. Red Wolf. Rinker. Romero. Roosevelt. Here it was. "Roosevelt, Casita—Lipan."

She opened it and saw that every doubt she had was justified. All her letters were there. The envelopes had been slit open, just like Eyota's. And worst or best of all, there was a tiny bundle of letters addressed to "Casita Smith" in Mollie's ornate handwriting. She traced the *C* of her name, feeling grateful. She had not been forgotten. Mollie could be trusted. She grabbed all the letters from her file and replaced the file

219

where she had found it. Taking a moment to catch her breath and smooth her hair, Casita forced herself to walk slowly. She kept it up until she reached the door, then burst into a run. Casita felt free and alone. It was good not to be marching in unison with the other girls. Past the dormitories, round the bandstand, she didn't stop until she reached the grove of cherry trees near the pond.

Everyone was in their assigned workshops and Miss Burgess was supervising the printing. No one would miss her for a little while. Heedless of any stains she might get on her grey dress, she climbed the largest tree and settled herself on a wide bough. She inhaled deeply the sweet smell of cherry blossoms, drowning out all the lies and deceptions.

She took Mollie's letters from her pocket. There were six. Mollie must be frantic worrying about her. Casita wondered what the school had told her. Sorting them from the earliest to the last, Casita read each one. A baby boy had come. He and Mollie were both well. They had named him Richard. Mollie missed Casita's corn stew. Charles was in charge of the regimental band now. Casita carefully tucked the letters in her pocket. She was going to read them again tonight and savor every word. The warmth of Mollie's love almost outweighed Casita's anger against Miss Mather. Almost but not quite.

She had been on her guard from the start, but the school had still lulled Casita into accepting her life here. She had walked straight into their trap because she wanted to draw in that studio and learn to make a newspaper. It had become easy for her to overlook the ways they controlled the children.

But everything was different now. Miss Mather had tried to keep Casita from her family. And they had wronged Eyota even more. Her father didn't even know she was sick. The school didn't love Indians, it hated them. Lieutenant Pratt and Miss Mather wouldn't be satisfied until every Indian was dead or "civilized."

She had been asleep, but now she was awake. They weren't going to kill this Ndé. They would not beat the Cuelcahen Ndé out of Casita. She might have to conceal herself as Casita Roosevelt, a docile student. But that was the Ndé way, too. Casita was a survivor.

The print shop would be missing her by now, but she stayed in the tree. Decisions had to be made. Should she tell Jack what Miss Mather had done? Would he care? He was happy being Miss Mather's favorite. He was excited to travel to Florida. It might be kinder to let him be.

But what about Eyota? Casita was afraid that Eyota was not strong enough to hear the truth. It would be better if Casita could find a way to send Eyota's last letter, still in her pocket. She could add a note of her own explaining why they had not been sent earlier. How could she do that? She had no stamps or envelopes. Well, she didn't have to decide right now. She swung down from the tree and circled around the quad to get back to the print shop.

Miss Burgess was damp with perspiration as she hovered

over the boys running the press. When she saw Casita, she frowned. "Where have you been?"

Without a qualm, Casita lied. "One of the teachers needed my help moving some books. I'm sorry I took so long."

"We have the first two hundred printed. You have a neat hand, so I want you to start addressing the envelopes for the subscribers."

There were two lists of subscribers. The first was of donors, politicians, local businesses—anyone who could support the school with money or supplies. A second list contained the parents of the students on the reservations. Could it be this simple? She scanned the second list until she saw Chief Flying Hawk's name. She wrote out his address on an envelope and then slipped in Eyota's letter along with the newspaper. Carlisle would pay the postage for her. Miss Burgess had no reason to open the envelope. Eyota's father would soon know everything. Casita wouldn't tell Eyota what she had done—it would do more harm than good to raise her hopes.

Tonight Casita would write a letter to Mollie and send it the same way. Miss Mather wouldn't suspect anything. It felt good to fire a round against the enemy.

❖

When Casita returned to her room after work, Nelly was sobbing on her bed.

"Nelly! What's wrong?" Casita rushed to her side.

"Eyota is in the infirmary. She fell to the floor while she

was sewing. She started to cough up blood."

Casita held Nelly tightly. Blood was never good. It meant that Eyota's illness had worsened. "She'll be fine," she said, rubbing Nelly's back.

"No she won't," sobbed Nelly. "My uncle caught the coughing disease after the soldiers came. He coughed blood one week and he died the next."

"She's stronger than you think. She's not going to die." Casita's protest sounded weak to her own ears. Wishing for something did not make it so. "Dr. Granger will take care of her."

"But what if the Indaa medicine doesn't work?"

"It has to," Casita said. They both turned to look at Eyota's empty bed. Her walls and chest were bare, because she had never wanted to treat this place like home. If she died, it would be like she had never been there.

"What if we found an Indian medicine man?"

Casita shook her head. "Lieutenant Pratt would never agree to that."

"I wish we knew healing," Nelly said.

"Me, too," Casita said. "My mother would have taught me after my Changing Woman ceremony." She caught her breath. The ceremony! She'd always been told that if she honored the Changing Mother Goddess, the Goddess would grant her healing powers. She could cure Eyota. Before she saw those letters in Miss Mather's office, Casita would never have thought of the Changing Woman ceremony. But now, it felt necessary, and natural, to return to the Ndé ways. To become one with the Ndé's goddess seemed to be the only way to fight the school's campaign to kill the Indian in all of them.

"What if I do the ceremony?" Casita asked. She knew Nelly's people, the Mescalero, had a similar ritual, although her people called the Goddess the White Painted Woman.

"Then you could heal her!" Nelly said, suddenly optimistic. "But she is Sioux—will the White Painted Woman help her?"

"Of course. Eyota is an Indian and she is our friend."

"But you are already a woman . . ." Casita could hear the doubt mixed with hope in Nelly's voice.

"I started the bleeding a year ago," Casita said. "But if the tribe had been at war or moving hunting grounds, we would have had to wait to do the ceremony anyway."

"Could we really do it?" Nelly looked at her with eyes that reminded her of Juanita. If Casita did the Changing Woman ceremony, it would not just be for herself and Eyota—it would be for Nelly too. The ceremony might help her remember that she was really Lenna of the Mescalero Apache.

"Why not?" Casita said. "I can ask Hazel to be my attendant." The attendant was usually an older woman who guided the young woman through the elaborate ceremony. It was an honor to be asked. They would be punished if they were caught, but Casita thought Hazel might welcome the chance to perform the ancient duty. "But we'll have to find all the things we need." She pulled out a piece of paper and pen

224

to list them, then thought better of it. If someone found the list, it would be used against her and her friends. Instead she drew a cane. A cattail with a dusting of pollen. Eagle feathers. What could be more innocent than a page of idle sketches? Then she drew the outlines of a dress; it should be yellow. It brought back powerful memories of her mother's strong hands rubbing the buckskin over and over for hours.

"The other Apaches will help," Nelly said confidently. "And I'll ask your brother." She hopped off the bed and went to Eyota's trunk. "And look!" She pulled out a dress that Eyota had just made. It was dark blue, but she had found some bright yellow fabric to trim the collar and the cuffs. "Don't we need a seashell, too?"

Casita smiled slowly. "We have one." She pulled out her necklace from the trunk and fastened it around her neck. "My necklace is abalone." How had Mollie known that Casita would need this one day? Casita was pleased that Mollie could play a small part in this ceremony.

"Maybe we can do it!" Nelly hugged Casita.

"If the school catches us, we'll all be punished," Casita warned. She might have decided the school was the enemy, but Nelly loved it here. Casita couldn't let Nelly get into trouble.

"Then we won't get caught," Nelly said. "I like eating, but I'll starve if we can help Eyota."

225

Nde'

CHAPTER TWENTY-THREE

ONCE CASITA HAD DECIDED TO DO THE CHANGING WOMAN ceremony, it became a conspiracy involving many people, even some strangers.

First Casita had to persuade Hazel to be her attendant. Hazel was the oldest Apache at Carlisle and Casita's friend. But she was still reluctant at first. "I don't know how to do everything the attendant does," she worried. "I might get it wrong."

"You are the best we have. You are the only one who has already done the ceremony." Casita was adamant. "Besides, we have to trust the Goddess. She knows where we are and how the school is against us. She will forgive the shortcuts we have to take."

"Are you sure about this, Casita?" Hazel asked. "You know what could happen." She didn't mention the beating, because Nelly was there.

"I'm sure," Casita said. "I have been away from the Ndé for too long."

"And it might help Eyota," Nelly added.

"Then I will help."

Normally the ceremony would last four days, but they could never manage that. The students were constantly watched by the teachers and they weren't allowed to leave the school grounds.

"We have to find a way to slip away," Casita insisted. She turned to Nelly. "Is there a teacher dinner coming up? A special guest? Anything that would keep the teachers busy for a little while?"

Nelly worked in the kitchen—the perfect place for her, since she was always hungry—so she always knew about any special meals that were coming up. Nelly considered. "Mrs. Pratt's birthday is next Saturday," she said. "All the teachers are invited to the lieutenant's house for cake."

Casita glanced at Hazel. "They'd be there for what, an hour? Would that be enough time?"

"I suppose it will have to be," Hazel said.

"Then next Saturday," Casita said. "And we can go to the cherry grove. That's out of sight of Pratt's house."

"We're going to do it!" Nelly jumped up and grabbed Casita's hands and twirled with her around the small room.

All her friends had a picture list of items they needed. The way her friends had come together reminded Casita of El Remolino. The women in the band would work so hard to prepare an agave roast or harvest the corn.

First on Casita's list was the dress. She had visited Eyota in the infirmary. She had told her friend everything about the ceremony except the healing part. Although she was weak and pale, Eyota had been eager to help.

"I only wish I could be there, too," Eyota said. The effort to talk was almost too much as a cough racked her body.

Casita had to cut a morning star and crescent moon from yellow cloth and sew them onto the skirt of Eyota's dark blue dress. The morning star represented the Goddess as she first appeared in the East, as a beautiful young woman. Then she moved westward, to disappear as she grew old, like the moon thinning until it faded away.

Nelly was in charge of the cane and the bells. "What are the bells for?" Nelly asked. "I never knew." Her people were not allowed to have the ceremony on their reservation.

"I'll sew them into the hem of the dress and we'll decorate the cane with them. They sound like rain, which gives life," Casita said. "Not that we ever had much rain in El Remolino. Nelly, have you found a cane yet?"

"Jack asked one of the Nez Perce boys to carve one in the woodworking shop," Nelly said. "The teacher there sleeps half the time and he won't notice."

"Ask him if he has any friends in the tinsmith shop who can make the bells," Casita said.

"It sure is lucky for us that Carlisle has all these workshops," Hazel said slyly. They all burst into laughter, loving the idea that Carlisle—a place dedicated to stamping out their beliefs—would provide the tools for the Apache ritual.

One of the most important ingredients for the ceremony was cattail pollen. Hazel and Nelly had woken early for three mornings in a row to sneak out to the pond to collect the pollen.

"How much is enough?" Casita asked, as she scraped the pollen off a cattail into a mason jar.

"We need as much as we can to bless Eyota," Hazel answered.

Casita was particularly grateful to Jack. She had wondered if he would help. He had embraced life at the school and prided himself on following the rules.

At first he had balked. "You'll get us all in trouble, Sister," he had said.

"So?" she challenged. "Jack Castro of the Lipan Apache would not have hesitated." She saw his forehead crinkle in a frown and she pressed the argument. "Do you remember at Fort Clark how much you wanted to continue your warrior training?"

"Yes," he said slowly. "But I found a way to do it without breaking the rules."

"The ceremony is just as important to me as your training was to you. But I don't have any other way to do it." She explained how sick Eyota was. "What if the Changing Woman Ceremony is her only hope?" She laid her hand on his. "I need your help."

Looking embarrassed, he said, "I didn't know you even wanted the ceremony. You never said anything."

"You wouldn't have heard me even if I had," Casita said ruefully. "You were too busy with the soldiers. And now you are called Jack Mather."

After a moment, he nodded. "No matter what my name is, I'll always be Ndé and I'll always be your brother. I'll do whatever's needed now."

He had already helped by recruiting his friends in the workshops to make what was needed, but there was a traditional role he could play in the ceremony.

"Guard us and keep us from harm during the ceremony," Casita told him.

"I can do that," he said with a grin.

❖

Finally Saturday evening came. Casita was strangely calm as Nelly and Hazel dressed her. She couldn't help thinking of how this should have been—her mother and aunts with her. Jack and the other boys standing guard outside the tent. The entire band waiting to honor her journey into adulthood. That version of her life had been shattered by that first gunshot at El Remolino, but she believed that somewhere her mother's spirit knew what Casita was about to do and approved.

Hazel brushed Casita's hair, parted it in the center, and let the rest hang loose down her back. Then she lifted the jingling dress over her head. Next, she smeared white clay on her face.

"You see why we call her the White Painted Woman?" Nelly said.

Casita tried to smile, but the clay was already hardening on her skin. Hazel tied Casita's necklace around the top of her head so the abalone shell lay flat on her forehead. It felt right that her father's gift be used today. That reminded Casita of an important part of the ritual—giving gifts to her attendants. "I have something for both of you," she said. Casita didn't have much at Carlisle, but she had drawn each of them a picture. Hazel's was a landscape with a lone rider silhouetted on a mountaintop.

Her voice choked, Hazel said, "It looks like home."

For Nelly, Casita had drawn a picture of her and her new friends. A wide smile rewarded her efforts.

"Now before it is time to go, you must eat," Hazel said. She opened a pot from the kitchen and took out a strawberry. "It really should be a cactus fruit, but they're hard to find in Pennsylvania."

"You brought food into the dorm?" Casita teased. She'd never forgotten that first night when Hazel had scolded Nelly for bringing an apple back to the dorm.

"It's part of the ceremony," Hazel said sternly. She sprinkled pollen on the strawberry and offered it to Casita. Casita reached to take it, but Hazel snatched it away. She did this three more times, then placed the strawberry on Casita's tongue. "This will make sure you always have an appetite."

"I'm always hungry," Nelly said. "Are there any more strawberries for me?"

Their laughter spoiled the solemnity of the moment, but Casita didn't mind. It seemed right that she should laugh with friends as she moved into adulthood.

A small rock hit their window. "That's Jack's signal," Nelly said. "The teachers are arriving. Hurry!" She rushed out to fetch the others. Hazel led Casita down the back stairs, slipping out the back door. They had invited only a few Apaches they could trust. Casita moved as gently as she could, but she still jangled loudly as she walked. No one appeared and Casita knew the Goddess must be on her side tonight.

When they came to the cherry tree grove, there were ten children waiting in the circle. To Casita's delight and surprise, Eyota arrived a moment later. Jack was pushing her in a wheeled chair.

Hazel instructed Casita to kneel in the center. She carried a little sack, and from it she took a jar of pollen. "This is for the strength a Ndé woman needs to bear children and protect the tribe," she said, smearing pollen on Casita's scalp where the hair was parted and then across the bridge of her nose.

Then she pulled out three eagle feathers.

"Where did . . ." Casita began, but she shushed when Hazel put a finger to her lips.

"Your brother borrowed them from Miss Mather's collection," she whispered. Maybe that was why Usen and the Goddess had brought Miss Mather into Jack's life. The ways of the gods were mysterious, Casita thought.

Hazel displayed the feather to the audience and said,

"This feather will hover over her for all of her life, protecting her from evil." She fixed that one to Casita's head. "And these shall grant her strength to carry the tribe's burdens." She placed one feather on each shoulder.

Hazel held out her hand. Jack stepped forward and presented her with a wooden cane decorated with little bells. Hazel handed it to Casita.

Hazel beckoned to Casita to stand. "Now do what I do," she said. Hazel lifted one foot and then stomped it on the ground. Casita followed. "When you put your foot back on the ground, hit the cane in the dirt." For the next twenty minutes, Casita stomped in time with Hazel. The only sounds were her feet hitting the ground and the jingling of her dress and cane. Her brother and friends danced, too. This was the dance she had practiced long ago that morning in El Remolino. It had taken over three years, but she was finally doing the Changing Woman dance.

At the end of the dance, Casita stood panting at one end of the grove. Hazel handed her the jar of pollen. The others lined up, Jack first. He dipped his finger in the pollen and then touched her face. She returned the blessing. "Good luck and long life." She hated that he would go soon to Florida; she hoped he would be happy. But now she didn't worry that he would be lost to her; he was still Ndé.

Nelly was next. She was so proud of herself for helping Casita perform the ritual. Casita hoped she could do the same thing for Nelly one day when it was her turn.

Eyota was the last one to come to Casita. Instead of speaking her blessing, Casita embraced her. She had saved most of the pollen to smear on her friend's thin arms and face.

"For good luck and long life, my friend," she said. "Be well." She felt something swelling in her heart. Maybe it was the Goddess filling Casita and letting her heal Eyota. Or it might have been gratitude to her friends, who had risked so much to help her become a woman in the ancient tradition of the Ndé. In either case, she felt as though she had finally come home.

AUTHOR'S NOTE

W HEN I STARTED RESEARCHING THE CARLISLE INDIAN INDUSTRIAL
School, I was looking for a compelling story. Since over 11,000
students came through Carlisle, I felt confident I could find
one. I got lucky right away when I found a documentary
called *The Lost Ones: Long Journey Home* on YouTube. It told
the story of two children, Casita and Jack, who had been torn
away from their Lipan Apache family during a massacre in the
1870s and eventually brought to be "civilized" at the Carlisle
boarding school. It was a great story and I really wanted to
tell it. But even though Casita and Jack are long dead, I knew
this story was important to their surviving family. I needed
their permission before I could start.

I reached out on Facebook to Richard Gonzales, Vice
Chairman of the Lipan Band of Texas, and asked if he would
talk with me. Richard is a retired policeman from San Jose

and he is spending his retirement researching his people. We met in person at a powwow in Georgetown, Texas. We talked for hours about Casita and Jack—but also about the other strong women in his family. Richard had pictures mounted on poster board in his pickup truck, and we looked at images of his family as he related to me their stories. I was delighted when he gave me his blessing to write about his ancestors. (Actually, Casita and Jack aren't his direct ancestors—he is the descendent of their cousin, Juanita.) He suggested I call his cousin, Daniel Romero, the Chairman of the Lipan Band of Texas. Daniel is the official historian of the family and he also gave me his blessing. Both gentlemen answered many questions as I wrote, giving me confidence to tackle Casita's incredible story.

LIPAN APACHE OR NDÉ

Apache Indian is a general term that encompasses several groups, including the Lipan Apache. The Lipan also called themselves Ndé. I preferred to use their own name for themselves in *The Lost Ones* because that is how Casita would have identified herself. The Lipan were composed of many bands. A "band" was several extended families traveling and living together. Lipan Apache occupied southeastern Texas and northern Mexico. They were fierce fighters, but also survivors. They hid when they needed to and were excellent at blending into their environment.

All their skills ultimately were no match for the overwhelming American forces sent against them in the 1870s and 1880s. The new state of Texas seized lands that had traditionally been held by the Lipan and then brought in the US Army to protect the settlers.

One Lipan band retreated across the Rio Grande into Mexico and established a base along the San Rodrigo River near the village of El Remolino in the early 1860s. They conducted raids on the Texas side of the border, stealing horses and often killing Texas settlers. Over a ten-year period, they caused an estimated $48,000,000 worth of property damage (measured in today's dollars). Whenever they were chased by US troops, they simply crossed the Rio Grande and taunted their pursuers from the Mexican side of the border.

The 4th Cavalry was stationed at Fort Clark. They had private instructions to deal with the "Indian problem" once and for all. Even though it was illegal for US troops to cross the border, the 4th dared to conduct multiple raids into Mexico. The first one was on May 17, 1873, when 400 men, guided by Seminole scouts, traveled over 140 miles in just 40 hours. Several villages in El Remolino were destroyed and 40 prisoners captured. We have a firsthand account from Captain Carter, one of the officers in charge of the raid. I took the liberty of making Carter a character in *The Lost Ones*. He represents the voice of the US Army in the book.

In *The Lost Ones*, Casita and Jack are taken prisoner on a similar raid in 1877. That raid wasn't documented, so I borrowed the details from the more famous raid in 1873. The rest of the prisoners were taken to a reservation, but Casita and Jack stayed behind at Fort Clark. It was at this point that their family lost track of the children.

Casita and her cousin Juanita never knew what happened to each other. But Juanita did survive, and Richard told me her story. When the soldiers raided the camp, Juanita hid with her little brother in a hole under some brush. The band had several hideouts like this prepared in case of danger. Maybe Miguel cried or Juanita moved, but for some reason one of the soldiers stabbed at their hiding place with his saber. The sharp blade killed little Miguel and pierced Juanita in the shoulder. She was brave enough not to cry out, and the soldier moved on.

Later, Juanita and another survivor, her brother Calixtro, walked 300 miles to San Juan, Texas. There they were reunited with their father, Casita's uncle, Juan Carlos. He had feared his whole family was dead, so he was grateful to find any survivors. He decided that it was too dangerous for any of them to be Lipan Apache. The family fled deeper into Mexico or to California, giving up their Apache names, culture, and history.

Juanita kept her Apache blood a secret even from her own family. She only told one of her daughters the story, who in turn told her daughter. Richard told me how Juanita's granddaughter "broke the news" to the family in the 1960s that they were Lipan Apache. After the initial shock, most of the family embraced their heritage, although some chose not to. Hundreds of people attend the annual family reunion and Richard likes to remind all of them that they would not exist if Juanita had not been so brave.

FORT CLARK

Fort Clark, the home of the 4th Cavalry, was an important military outpost in southeastern Texas. Casita and Jack were taken in by a military man and his wife, Lt. Charles and Mollie Smith. In real life, the Smiths traveled from base to base—Charles had a position with the military marching band—but for *The Lost Ones* I kept them stationed at Fort Clark.

We know very little about the Smiths, so I took the liberty of making Mollie a Quaker and a nurse. As a nurse, Mollie can meet Casita in the hospital. As a Quaker, she is interested in social justice and is a pacifist. Up to the Civil War, the Quakers were vocal abolitionists. After slavery was abolished with the ratification of the Thirteenth Amendment in 1865, the Quakers found a new cause: a humane solution to the Indian problem. Mollie takes in two Indian children, despite the disapproval of her military husband, to prove the Quaker theory that the Indians can be won over with kindness. Naturally she clashes with the military establishment, which is dedicated to eliminating Indians, either by sending them to reservations or by killing them.

Casita and Jack lived with the Smiths for almost three years. The Smith family has preserved a picture of the two children. On the back, Charles wrote: "Casita and Jack Smith—they always address Mollie as dear Mamma." This implies that they thought of themselves as a family. In *The Lost Ones*, I have Charles getting this photograph taken in San Antonio just before they board the train to Carlisle.

In 1880, the Commanding Officer of Fort Clark was asked to send students to the new Indian school in Carlisle, PA. Since Casita and Jack were still officially "prisoners of war," it was within his discretion to send them. We can only guess that it was a difficult separation for all of them. The Smiths would never see Casita and Jack again.

Caleb was not a real person, but the anger he feels toward the Apache was typical. Seminole Jim is based on a true person. The Seminole scouts were valued members of the Fort Clark community, although they lived just outside the fort. They were excellent trackers and strong fighters. They worked for the US Army because they had been promised land and citizenship. However, the US government failed to keep this promise.

CARLISLE INDIAN INDUSTRIAL SCHOOL

Founded in 1879 by Captain Richard Henry Pratt, Carlisle was the first off-reservation Indian boarding school paid for by the US government. It was built on the site of a former Army barracks in Carlisle, PA. Pratt believed that Native Americans could be "civilized" and become useful citizens. His informal motto was "Kill the Indian, Save the Man." Pratt believed that if the Indians learned English and

Colonel Richard Henry Pratt, the founder of the Carlisle Indian Industrial School, in 1901

a trade, they could be useful members of American society. Upon arrival at Carlisle, students' hair was cut and their names were changed. Students were forbidden to speak their own language or practice their own religion. The school was run like a military regiment with much marching and strict discipline, including corporal punishment. Students had regular classwork in the morning and they learned a trade in the afternoon. Pratt also had an outing program for students to leave the school during the summers and work at local farms or homes. The boys did agricultural work and the girls served as domestic servants.

Carlisle became the model for 26 Bureau of Indian Affairs boarding schools in 15 states and territories. From 1879 until 1918, almost 12,000 Native American children from 140 tribes

ABOVE: This photograph of Apache students from Fort Marion, Florida, was taken as they arrived at the school in the late 1800s, early 1900s.
BELOW: These Carlisle students were photographed after they arrived at the school in the late 1800s, early 1900s.

ABOVE: A clothes-mending class in 1901.
BELOW: The school's infirmary in 1901.

ABOVE: The metalworking workshop in 1904.
BELOW: The printing shop in the early 1900s.

attended Carlisle; however, according to one source, only 8% of the students graduated. Many students simply returned home after a time; others ran away. Hundreds became ill and died. There is a student cemetery at Carlisle today housing 175 graves, but many children's bodies were sent home to their families.

Today most historians, especially among the Native American community, feel the Carlisle Indian Industrial School represents a shameful attempt to brainwash Indian children. Often the children had no choice about coming to Carlisle, and once there they suffered terribly from being forced to renounce their culture and language.

On the other hand, many students loved the school. They were grateful for the opportunity to be educated and even sent their own children there. Many students corresponded with Pratt for many years and spoke highly of their time at Carlisle.

The school had a deliberate policy to separate students who were from the same tribe. However, in the records, Jack and Casita are listed as "Lipan." Other students are identified as "Apache." I used this sloppy recordkeeping to find a way to keep Casita and Lenna/Nelly in the same room.

One of the ways that Pratt publicized his school's accomplishments was through a newspaper, produced by the faculty and students at Carlisle. The newspaper had several names, but was called *Eadle Keahtah Toh* when Casita was there. Pratt and Miss Burgess saw the newspaper as a tool for propaganda.

Every article conveys the message that the Indian students are better off at Carlisle. The article that appears in the second edition of the paper is one of the few references we find at Carlisle to Casita. Here is an excerpt from the article:

> *On examination we found three large scars on Casita, one on her head, one on the back, and one on the front of her shoulder. When questioned as to how the scars came to be there, she said it was when her mother tried to kill her with a rock. This seemed almost incredible so we said, "What your own mother?" "Yes, ma'am," she replied. "But why did she do that?" we asked and the answer was "so as to keep the white men from getting me in the fight." Then we understood, for we had heard before, of mothers doing such deeds of horror when they found the result of the battle would be against them. After some further talk with her, we asked if she would rather have gone back to her mother than to have come here, but she said "No, my mother is dead."*

Lenna and Eyota are invented characters. In *The Lost Ones*, Lenna is grateful to be at Carlisle. Conditions on her reservation were so poor that she finds Carlisle to be a safe haven. This positive attitude was typical of many children who came to Carlisle. Their parents sent them to Pennsylvania not only to receive an education, but also so they would be fed and clothed. Eyota represents the opposite point of view. She is the daughter of a Sioux chief. She resents the US Army for sending her to Carlisle as a hostage for her father's good behavior. Her story was partly inspired by Maud Swift Bear, one of the first children to die at Carlisle. Like Eyota, she arrived at the school with a respiratory disease. Her father was an important Sioux chief. Lieutenant Pratt stressed in his letter to her father that Maud had arrived with bad lungs and there was nothing the school could have done.

Jack was adopted by Miss Mather. She brought him to St. Augustine, Florida. He got tuberculosis while he was there, returned to Carlisle in 1888, and died when he was around 18 years old.

We have no way of knowing if Casita ever performed her Changing Woman dance, but I like to think that she did. Certainly she did not excel as a student at Carlisle: her reports indicate that she was an average student. After a few years, she was sent out to work for a local family as a servant. She would do this for a few years, then return to Carlisle before finding a new position. Officially, she remained a student at Carlisle until her death in 1906, around the age of 39. During her final illness, she was cared for by a Quaker community. She is buried in a Quaker cemetery about 140 miles from Carlisle and almost 2,000 miles from El Remolino. She left behind a two-year-old son named Richard, although there is no record of a marriage or who the father was.

Since Casita was still officially a student at Carlisle, Richard was taken in by the school. He was the youngest student they ever had. He was adopted by a well-to-do family in town, but continued to have strong ties to Carlisle until it closed in 1917. He was reportedly friends with the famous athlete Jim Thorpe, who played football at Carlisle. Although he married, Richard never had children. He was the third and last Lipan Apache at the Carlisle School.

In *The Lost Ones*, Casita never knows what happened to her father. We do know from Juanita's descendants that he never stopped looking for his children, although he died a few years after the raid.

Juanita's descendants never forgot the missing children. They never thought to look for them at Carlisle, 1,800 miles away from where they were last seen. And even if they had, the children had undergone several name changes. It took a visiting British scholar to piece together the story. In 2000, Dr. Jacqueline Fear-Segal came to Carlisle to study Native American history. She came across Casita's name in the records about Carlisle maintained by the Cumberland Valley Historical Society. She contacted Daniel Romero of the Lipan Band of Texas to ask for more information. Daniel, the leader of the band, was surprised and delighted to finally discover the fate of the lost children. In 2009, on the anniversary of the attack on El Remolino, Daniel and Richard, accompanied by other Lipans, came to Carlisle to offer blessings at the gravesites of Jack and Casita, welcoming the children back to the tribe. They are no longer lost.

AN AFTERWORD

THE HISTORY OF THE NDÉ CAN BE DOCUMENTED AS FAR BACK AS the 1500s. Every year for centuries the Ndé (Lipan Apache) met as a Nation on the third Saturday of August, timed to coincide with the annual pre-winter hunt. This gathering was when marriages, births, and new leaders were celebrated. This tradition continues today with the descendants of the first Lipan. An annual reunion still brings hundreds of our family together. At one such gathering in 1980, I was given the honor of being my family's historian. Until then, our family's history had been an oral history; I was the first to write it down.

One of the darkest days in our history was May 18, 1873, when the US 4th Cavalry, without orders, crossed the Rio Grande and attacked the Lipan Apache villages, massacring many Ndé. This raid was followed by many more. Casita and Jack were taken prisoner in such a raid. Their cousins Juanita and Calixtro escaped the soldiers.

Juanita Castro, who is my ancestor, moved to the border-land frontier city of Laredo and married Jesus Cavazos, a Spanish Land Grant property owner. She lived a long life and had thirteen children and many grandchildren and great-grandchildren. If she had not been so brave on the day of that raid, none of these people would ever have been born. Calixtro also had children and had the distinction of becoming a third-generation Texas Ranger.

Although Juanita and Calixtro hid their heritage, they never forgot Casita and Jack, passing on their story in secret to their children and grandchildren.

At the annual reunions, a special plate was prepared. We called this a "grandfather's plate" to honor those we had lost. We would pray for them and then tip the food into the fire. Our people could not move forward until our lost ones were sent home.

We were very happy to know what had become of Jack and Casita. Casita has the distinction of being the longest serving "Woman Prisoner of War" and longest enrolled student of the Carlisle Indian Industrial School. In 2009, on the anniversary of the raid, we went to Pennsylvania to say prayers for our lost children and to ask the creator to open the door and let them in.

For over one hundred and fifty years, the story told about our people ignored what truly happened to them as the US military progressed westward. Our indigenous way of life became a struggle for survival. Casita's story captures the struggles of so many Ndé both before and after her death. Now that her story has been told, the Ndé believe that her captivity was not in vain; her life had meaning. Her story not only condemns the Carlisle School's system of values, but also challenges our morals as a nation. But most importantly, in her heart, Casita managed to journey home to the Ndé.

Daniel Castro Romero, Jr.

RESOURCES

Adams, David Wallace. *Education for Extinction: American Indians and the Boarding School Experience, 1875–1928.* Lawrence, KS: University Press of Kansas, 1995.

Ball, Eve, with Nora Henn and Lynda A. Sánchez. *Indeh: An Apache Odyssey.* Norman, OK: University of Oklahoma Press, 1988.

Carter, Robert. *On the Border with MacKenzie, or Winning West Texas from the Comanches.* Austin, TX: Texas State Historical Association, 2011.

Churchill, Ward. *Kill the Indian, Save the Man: The Genocidal Impact of American Indian Residential Schools.* San Francisco: City Lights Books, 2004.

Fear-Segal, Jacqueline. *White Man's Club: Schools, Race, and the Struggle of Indian Acculturation.* Lincoln: University of Nebraska Press, 2007.

Golston, Sydele. *Changing Woman of the Apache: Women's Lives in Past and Present.* New York: Franklin Watts, 1996.

Haenn, William. *Fort Clark and Brackettville: Land of Heroes.* Images of America Series. Charleston, SC: Arcadia Publishing, 2002.

Haley, James. *Apaches: A History and Culture Portrait.* Norman, OK: University of Oklahoma Press, 1981.

Minor, Nancy McGown. *Turning Adversity to Advantage: A History of the Lipan Apaches of Texas and Northern Mexico, 1700–1900.* Lanham, MD: University Press of America, 2009.

Pirtle, Caleb. *The Lonely Sentinel: Fort Clark, on Texas's Western Frontier.* Austin, TX: Eakin Press, 1985.

Pratt, Richard Henry. *Battlefield and Classroom: Four Decades with the American Indian, 1867–1904.* New Haven, CT: Yale University Press, 1964.

Robinson, Sherry. *Apache Voices: Their Stories of Survival As Told to Eve Ball.* Albuquerque, NM: University of New Mexico Press, 2000.

Stockel, Henrietta. *Women of the Apache Nation: Voices of Truth.* Reno, NV: University of Nevada Press, 1991.

Trafzer, Clifford, ed. *Boarding School Blues: Revisiting American Indian Educational Experiences.* Lincoln, NE: University of Nebraska Press, 1996.

Witmer, Linda. *The Indian Industrial School, Carlisle, Pennsylvania 1879–1918.* Carlisle, PA: Cumberland County Historical Society, 1993.

FURTHER READING *

Most of my sources were academic books meant for adults. However, some books and websites that are more appropriate for young people are listed below:

Carvell, Marlene. *Sweetgrass Basket.* New York: Dutton Children's Books, 2005.
A historical novel in prose poetry, this is the story of two young sisters at Carlisle. One of the few accounts of girls at the school.

*websites active at time of publication

Community Studies Center at Dickinson College. *The Lost Ones: Long Journey Home.* https://www.youtube.com/watch?v=_I4jF22bXeA.
This excerpt of a documentary by the Community Studies Center at Dickinson College tells the story of Casita and Jack, as well as the Carlisle School. You can see Daniel Romero and his uncle Richard Gonzalez discussing how they brought Casita and Jack home.

Cooper, Michael. *Indian School: Teaching the White Man's Way.* New York: Clarion Books, 1999.
This is a nonfiction book that explores the Indian schools, especially Carlisle. There are lots of pictures.

Friends of the Fort Clark Historic District. 2016. http://www.ffchd.org.
This is the website of the Friends of Fort Clark Historic District. It is full of interesting information about the fort, including maps and pictures of life at the fort in the 1870s.

Landis, Barbara. Carlisle Indian Industrial School History. 1996. http://home.epix.net/~landis/histry.html.
Cumberland Valley Historical Society researcher Barbara Landis has developed a website about the history of the Carlisle School.

Ramos, Mary G. "Family Life at the Forts." Texas Almanac. http://texasalmanac.com/topics/history/family-life-forts-0.
This website from the Texas State Historical Association has great information about life for families at the forts.

Standing Bear, Luther. *My People, the Sioux.* Lincoln, NE: Bison Books, 2006.
Luther Standing Bear was one of the first students at Carlisle and one of the school's success stories. Originally published in 1928, this autobiography is the perfect way to see Carlisle as it was at the beginning.

Texas Historical Commission. Fort Griffin: State Historic Site. http://www.visitfortgriffin.com/index.aspx?page=898.
This is a website about a fort similar to Fort Clark with great information about the daily life of a soldier in the 1870s.

Welker, Glenn. "Lipan Apache (Tindi)." Indians.org. http://www.indians.org/welker/lipanap.htm.
This website has a history of Casita's family, based on research done by Daniel Castro Romero.

PHOTO CREDITS

Cumberland County Historical Society, Carlisle, PA: 2.

The Granger Collection, New York: 242 (top and bottom).

Library of Congress, Prints and Photographs Division: LC-USZ62-26798: 241; LC-USZ62-26792: 243 (top); LC-USZ62-26796: 243 (bottom); LC-USZ62-112855: 244 (top); LC-DIG-ggbain-11206: 244 (bottom).

Courtesy of Daniel Castro Romero, Jr., General Council Chairman, Lipan Apache Band of Texas: 9.

PRAISE FOR THE
HIDDEN HISTORIES SERIES

Rory's Promise

"This first in the Hidden Histories series of middle-grade novels highlights an episode in which New. York City's Foundling Hospital sent white youth to unfamiliar Arizona Territory to be adopted by Mexican Catholics, raising the ire of Protestant Anglos and revealing the depths of their prejudice. . . . The injustice, drama and action will have readers riveted. . . . An exciting, eye-opening read." —*Kirkus Reviews*

"Rory is a likable protagonist with determination and heart, all of which will endear her to readers." —*Booklist*

"Readers will enjoy the fast-paced action and likable main character. This is a historical novel with a unique topic and plenty of substance, making it especially suitable for class or group discussion." —*School Library Journal*

FREEDOM'S PRICE

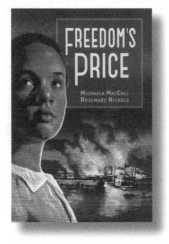

"Expect a savvy, energetic fighter in Eliza, and suspenseful plotting in this fine piece of historical fiction from the Hidden Histories series."

—*Booklist Online*

"History comes alive in this imagining of the life of Eliza Scott, one of the daughters of Dred Scott, the slave at the center of a landmark case in American history. . . . VERDICT: A great choice to support school curriculum."

—*School Library Journal*

"A fast-paced story with a strong female protagonist and a look at a little-known time period, this book is a good choice for historical fiction units and recreational reading. RECOMMENDED."

—*School Library Connection*